Also by
Carlton Mellick III

Satan Burger
Electric Jesus Corpse (Fan Club Exclusive)
Sunset With a Beard (stories)
Razor Wire Pubic Hair
Teeth and Tongue Landscape
The Steel Breakfast Era
The Baby Jesus Butt Plug
Fishy-fleshed
The Menstruating Mall
Ocean of Lard (with Kevin L. Donihe)
Punk Land
Sex and Death in Television Town
Sea of the Patchwork Cats
The Haunted Vagina
Cancer-cute (Fan Club Exclusive)
War Slut
Sausagey Santa
Ugly Heaven
Adolf in Wonderland
Ultra Fuckers
Cybernetrix
The Egg Man
Apeshit
The Faggiest Vampire
The Cannibals of Candyland
Warrior Wolf Women of the Wasteland
The Kobold Wizard's Dildo of Enlightenment +2
Zombies and Shit

THE BAD BOX

CARLTON MELLICK III

ERASERHEAD PRESS
PORTLAND, OREGON

ERASERHEAD PRESS
P.O. BOX 10065
PORTLAND, OR 97296

WWW.ERASERHEADPRESS.COM

ISBN: 978-1-62105-312-5

AUTHOR'S NOTE

What would a Carlton Mellick III *Goosebumps* book look like? This was going through my head when I sat down to write *The Bad Box*. Quite a few people have compared my books to the famous children's horror series, describing them as *Goosebumps for adults*. I'm not sure I would completely agree with this description, but I do find it both complimentary and absolutely hilarious. In fact, I would not be ashamed at all if I ended up being known as the R. L. Stine of bizarro fiction one day. The man wrote over three hundred books in his career, releasing about a dozen titles per year, and inspired an entire generation of child horror fans. He's a legend.

Although *The Bad Box* ended up being more a story about classism than a tribute to R. L. Stine, I still hope that it will appeal to those of you who have always wanted to know what I would have done with a *Goosebumps* book had I been hired to ghost-write one back in the day (if you didn't know, a good portion of those books were ghostwritten by established horror writers who have all been sworn to secrecy unless you catch them drunk at a convention party).

So here it is, *The Bad Box*, my sixty-first book release. I hope you enjoy it.

—Carlton Mellick III 3/3/2020 3:30pm

CHAPTER
ONE

There's nothing in the world that Benny Paulson hates more than taking tests. He's just terrible at them. The absolute worst test-taker in the whole school. It's not that he's a dumb kid who doesn't know how to study or pay attention in class. He actually gets nothing but good grades on all of his non-test school work. He regularly gets an A+ whenever he does a book report or essay or homework assignment. But he's not passed a single test all year.

His problem is that tests give him so much anxiety that he's not able to think straight. It's just too much pressure. Even if he knows absolutely everything there is to know on a particular subject he's still not capable of achieving a passing grade. He's lucky if he even answers all the questions before the time runs out. He just falls immediately into a panic the second a test begins and stares at the clock while the time tick-ticks away from him. It doesn't help that test-failers are allotted ten minutes less time than test-passers. It also doesn't help that all ten of his fingers have been magically transformed into live banana slugs and can barely hold up a pencil.

Benny's last test was an especially horrible one. He took it yesterday during math class, a test on division and multiplication, all easy stuff that he could do in his sleep, but due to the intense amount of pressure he just couldn't concentrate. All the numbers became blurry on his page. All the questions might as well have been written in Japanese. He tried his hardest but he knows that he had to have failed miserably. Even the answers he got right were probably marked as wrong due to his unreadable slug-finger handwriting.

Mrs. Gustafson is in the front of the classroom preparing to read off the test scores. She twiddles the papers with her bony fingers as she glares at each of her students. Her long curled boot taps adamantly against the hardwood floor, echoing like an annoyed metronome in everyone's ears. She doesn't look very happy with the test results. Mrs. Gustafson rarely ever looks happy with any test results.

"May I have everyone's attention, please?" she asks the class in her shrill witch-like voice.

All of the children quiver with anticipation. They can't wait to know how well they did on their math tests. Unlike Benny, several of them are very good at taking tests and try to do better every single time. They all want more than anything to get an A+ because getting an A+ is the most important thing in the world to them. Only the coolest, smartest, most popular kids in school ever get grades that good.

"Some of you did well…" Mrs. Gustafson tells the class. "But many of you could do much, much better."

Benny slinks in his chair as the teacher looks directly into his eyes. He knows he didn't do a good job. He didn't do a good job at all. Just like the last fourteen tests he's taken this year, Benny is sure that he failed again.

"We'll start with the best scores," says Mrs. Gustafson, looking down at the papers in her hand as she pushes her horn-rimmed reading glasses up her long pointed nose. "Three of you have received a perfect score. One hundred percent. And two received a 98."

The children gasp with excitement. They can't believe their ears. Five of them did that well? That's twenty percent of the class. There's never been that many to score that high before. Usually there's just two or three.

"All five A+ students will receive rewards from the good box," says Mrs. Gustafson.

The kids clap and cheer as the teacher pulls a glowing blue box out of her desk and places it on the table in front of her. When the children see it, their eyes widen with enthusiasm. The good box pulses with magic and wonder. It is small, no larger than a tissue box, yet it seems to be infinite, like it contains an entire universe within its tiny confines. It entrances the children, filling their eyes with hypnotic blue light, bringing an overwhelming sensation of warmth and peacefulness that embraces everyone in the room.

"The first person to receive their prize, with a score

of 100 percent, is Adam Brunner."

The entire classroom stands and claps for Adam. It's his first time receiving an A+ this year. The look on his face is one of shock and joy. He can't believe he actually got a perfect score on the math test.

"Really?" Adam cries. "I got a hundred?"

The teacher nods and waves him over.

Adam pumps his fist and accepts several high fives from his classmates as he makes his way to the front of the class. But he doesn't accept Benny's high five. Even though Adam is one of the nicest kids in the class, he won't go anywhere near Benny and his slug fingers.

"This is your first time with the good box, correct?" asks the teacher.

Adam nods his head.

"Well, congratulations," she says. "Now take your reward."

Adam looks down into the good box's opening, peering into the great magical void within. He cautiously puts his hand inside, both eager and fearful at the same time. The second his hand enters, the box glows brighter and hums like a microwave. Then a burst of light fills Adam's skin and puts a twinkle in his eyes.

"What did you get? What did you get?" the other kids scream.

Adam removes his hand from the box and says, "Wǒ xiànzài hěn cōngmíng."

After he says this, his eyes dart up at the teacher and he says, "Whoa! I learned Cantonese!"

Mrs. Gustafson puts on a fake smile and pats him on

the back. "Very good, Adam. Now go back to your seat."

"I can speak a foreign language!" he cries, running all the way back to his desk.

The other kids don't clap for him, unimpressed by his reward. Although instantly learning a new language would be an incredible gift that anyone would be happy to receive, the kids in their class think it's way too boring to get excited about it. Compared to many of the other gifts from the good box, it is quite lackluster.

"Zhè hěn bàng!" Adam yells.

Heidi is the next student to be called to the front of the room. She, too, has never received a gift from the good box before and can hardly contain her eagerness. Her reward is the complete opposite of Adam's—something that is far more interesting to the rest of the children, yet not at all useful in her daily life. She has been given the ability to shoot rainbows from her fingertips.

"So awesome!" the girls in the room cry as Heidi shoots rainbows at them.

The rainbows don't do anything but look pretty. Still, all the girls in the class are incredibly jealous of her. Although Heidi was always one of the most quiet, overlooked girls in the class, she'll surely be popular from this day forward. Everyone is going to want to play with her on the playground so that she can shoot rainbows at them.

"Very good, Heidi," says Mrs. Gustafson. "But there's no rainbow conjuring allowed in class."

Heidi can't resist shooting off one more rainbow before returning to her seat.

The two students who received 98 percent are Billy and Matty, two friends who always study together after school and tend to do well on tests, especially math and science tests. They have already received gifts from the good box this year—Billy with his stretchable arms and back-flipping skills and Matty with his ability to breathe underwater. It's no surprise that they'd be getting even more gifts than they had before.

"Whoa! I got x-ray vision!" Billy cries after he accepts his reward from the good box.

Mrs. Gustafson gives him a stern look. "Now, no using that on the girls, Billy."

But it's too late. Billy is already using his x-ray vision on all of the kids in class.

"It's okay, Mrs. Gustafson," Billy says. "All I can see is their bones."

"Cool!" the other kids cry.

"You're all skeletons!" Billy yells. "It looks like Halloween!"

Mrs. Gustafson sighs at the excited boy. "It doesn't matter, Billy. Bones are still private. No using x-ray vision in class. It's impolite."

Billy continues, staring at the boy in the front row, "Whoa! Greg's got bones made of metal! Why are your bones metal, Greg?"

Mrs. Gustafson yells, "I said no x-ray vision in class!"

When Matty receives his reward, the pudgy boy says, "I can walk through solid objects!" Matty passes through the table in front of him. "I'm like a ghost!"

The other kids clap and cheer for him.

On his way back to his seat, he takes the most direct route, cutting through the other students and desks and chairs.

Mrs. Gustafson scolds him. "No walking through your classmates, Matty. It's impolite."

The pudgy boy agrees and walks around the last kid in his path. He sits down in his seat and plays with his new power, dipping his hand through the surface of his desk to retrieve paperclips and erasers.

Everyone knows who the last person will be. It's Tracy Wilson, the smartest person in school. Tracy is the girl everyone in class wants to be friends with. She's the prettiest, the smartest, the most popular girl any of them have ever met. She's also the luckiest. As the very first person to get an A+ in Mrs. Gustafson's class, Tracy was the first of them to receive a reward from the good box. And her first reward was the best possible gift that anyone could ever receive: photographic memory.

Because Tracy now has a gift of perfect memory, she has an insanely unfair advantage over the other students. She's able to memorize entire textbooks within hours. She doesn't even need to study anymore. Because of this ability, she has been able to get 100% on every single test she has taken since. All fourteen of them. And she's been able to obtain new rewards from the good box after every single one.

Tracy already has an amazing assortment of gifts at this time and the year isn't even halfway over. Besides photographic memory, she also has super speed, super hearing, perfect eyesight, glow-in-the-dark skin, telekinesis, and the ability to grow into a giantess. She has mastered the arts of figure-skating, still-life painting, and sharp-shooting with a bow and arrow. She can even bend into shapes the human form was never meant to bend with her gift of super flexibility.

Benny is tragically in love with Tracy. Although everyone has fallen in love with her since she's obtained so many wonderful powers, Benny has loved her even before they entered the fifth grade. He's loved her since they were six years old and starting school together.

Tracy stands up from her seat and walks gracefully to the front of the room. Her icy pale skin glistens in the fluorescent lighting. Her large white-feathered angel wings sway like the tail of a wedding gown with every step she takes.

That is the gift she's always been most proud of, the gift everyone has always admired most about her: the angel wings. They were her second gift, won for

16

acing the first social studies test, and there's never been a person more deserving than she. Because Tracy *is* an angel. That's what Benny has always believed. With her snowy white skin, long white hair that flows down to her hips, and clear silver eyes that reflect everything she looks at like mirrors, everything about Tracy seems to be angelic to Benny.

Tracy was born an albino and was considered a freak to all the other kids when she first entered school. But she was never ashamed of her birth defect. She embraced it. She only wore all white dresses and white shoes and hats. Never adding a single drop of color to her look. Benny loved how her all-white appearance stood out from everyone else. He saw her as an angel in human form. And the day she gained her angel wings, Benny knew it was her destiny to become one.

"I didn't even call your name, Tracy," Mrs. Gustafson says to the girl with the angel wings.

Tracy looks at her and speaks with confidence. "Did I not score a hundred on the exam?"

The teacher shrugs. "Of course you did."

Tracy nods. "Very well."

When Tracy puts her hand into the good box, she blinks twice and allows a new power to enter her body.

"What did you get?" ask the girls in the front row.

"Hmmm…" Tracy says, examining her hands. "This is different…"

"What is it? What is it? What is it?" the other kids cry.

She pulls a few pieces of paper out of her pocket and says, "I can turn anything into money."

The pieces of paper instantly transform into thousand dollar bills.

The second they see this, all the children in the room squeal with envy.

"Anyone want some money?" Tracy asks.

All the kids raise their hands, yelling, "I want money! I want money!"

Tracy hands the three thousand dollars to the closest person to her and then touches the pencils of everyone within arm's reaching, turning their pencils into thousand dollar bills. The children scream with excitement.

"How come she always gets the best powers?" asks the girl in front of Benny.

"I know! It's so unfair!" shouts another girl.

As Tracy continues handing out thousands of dollars to each of her classmates, Mrs. Gustafson sighs and asks her to stop.

The teacher says, "Come on, Tracy. You should know better than that. You must use your gifts responsibly. If you go turning everything you touch into thousand dollar bills it will have a horrible impact on our economy. You should use this gift for financial emergencies only."

Tracy nods at the teacher and says, "Yes, Mrs. Gustafson," immediately ceasing the thousand dollar giveaways.

All the children who were not given any money sigh with disappointment. Especially Benny. Not because he didn't get his pencil turned into a thousand dollar bill, but because Tracy was just about to approach his desk and look him in the eyes. It's been a very long time since Tracy has looked him in the eyes. They used to sit next to each other just last year and sometimes talk or pass notes, but they haven't even been within three feet of each other this entire year. They used to be equals before Mrs. Gustafson's class. But now she is the goddess of the classroom and he is the lowest of the low.

Mrs. Gustafson puts away the good box, hiding it in the locked drawer at the bottom of her desk, and then brings out another box.

"Now for the students who did poorly on yesterday's test."

All the children cower at the sight of the second box. It is made of black steel, wrapped in barbed chains and covered in long pointed monstrous teeth. It hisses and growls in the teacher's hands, and oozes a thick dark fluid that smells of dead fish. Once the teacher places the box on the table, everyone in the room fills with dread and unease. The good box emanated the positive emotions of warmth and protection, but this box emits horrible emotions. It makes people feel confused and depressed and afraid. It is a very, very evil box.

"Which of you have failed this time?" asks the teacher, peering out at her students. "Which of you will receive punishment from the bad box?"

Everyone looks at Benny.

As the only person who has failed every single test of the year, Benny is an obvious candidate for the bad box.

In fact, he's usually the only person whoever fails any test. The other kids are so scared about being punished by the bad box that they always make sure to study as hard as they can and unlike Benny they never let their fear of failure freeze them up in the middle of answering questions. The extreme pressure helps them to focus, to try as hard as they can. That's why Mrs. Gustafson's class always has the best test results of any children in the school.

"I'm ashamed you are my student, Benjamin," the teacher says to him.

He lowers his ball bearing eyes. She doesn't need to call his name. He knows as well as everyone that he failed yet another test.

"Come get your punishment," she tells him.

Benny stands up on his hairy goat legs and clip-clops toward the front of the class. He's gotten fourteen punishments from the bad box and every single one of them has been worse than the last. Besides his weird ball bearing eyes that make him look like a metal robot, his wiggling slug fingers, and his goat legs, Benjamin has also been punished with a long scaly lizard tail, poor eye-hand coordination, attention deficit disorder, full body moles, early balding, the inability to see fast-moving objects, irritable bowel syndrome, and rotten egg smells. He really doesn't want to know what else he will be cursed with for the rest of the school year.

"It's your own fault, Benjamin," says the teacher. "If you only applied yourself and studied harder this wouldn't happen to you every single time."

Benny wants to explain himself. He wants to say that he studies as hard as he can, that he knows all the answers to every question, that he would be a straight-A student if only the punishment didn't give him so much anxiety. But he's too intimidated to speak up. Mrs. Gustafson scares him more than any teacher has ever scared him before.

"Go on, accept your punishment," the teacher says.

Benny looks down into the opening of the bad box. The lips are lined with razor-sharp teeth, like it's waiting to bite his hand off the second he puts it within. The inside of the box is an infinite depth of darkness and pain. It's like he's looking directly into the bowels of hell and has no choice but to put a part of himself into it.

As Benny stares down into the darkness, Mrs. Gustafson grows impatient. "Are you going to do it or do I have to force your hand in there?"

Benny snaps out of it and gives in. His teacher is the only thing scarier to him than the bad box. He doesn't want to make her angrier with him than she already is.

As he lowers his slug fingers through the toothy mouth of the horrible box, the oily wet interior sliding against the back of his hand, he trembles so much that his teeth begin to chatter, a trail of snot drips down his lips. Once his hand is all the way inside, an electric shock grips his body. His punishment is burned into his soul like a branding iron, permanently staining him with something horrible.

He immediately knows what he's been given. A deep, guttural voice tells him his punishment within the back of his head.

"Crickets," it tells him.

Benny freaks out. He feels them crawling all over him.

"Ahhhhh!" Benny screams. "I'm full of crickets!"

All the children burst into laughter as Benny pukes crickets from his mouth and pulls them from his nostrils.

"Cricket Boy!" Billy shouts, pointing and giggling at the freakish child. "We'll call him Cricket Boy!"

Benny hops and squirms as the little insects crawl inside his body. He pulls up his shirt with his slimy slugs, trying to brush them away, but the crickets can't be removed. They are beneath his skin, little bumps crawling inside of him, hopping and chirping as they try to escape.

"Serves you right, Benjamin," says Mrs. Gustafson. "Maybe this will teach you to do better next time."

Benny looks at his teacher. "But it's itchy!" he cries, rubbing the chirping lumps under his skin, crickets hopping out of his mouth between words. "It's so itchy!"

The other kids can't stop laughing at his misfortune. They already thought of him as an ugly, idiotic freak, but now he's even funnier to them. He's like a dancing clown. His pain and suffering brings them great joy.

Tracy is the only one who doesn't laugh at Benny's torment. Perhaps because she empathizes with him. Or perhaps she just has so much confidence in herself that she doesn't need to make fun of less fortunate kids in order to feel better about herself. Either way, it makes Benny feel slightly better to know at least one person is able to refrain from laughing at him. Her opinion is the only one that matters to him anyway.

Benny returns to his seat and squishes six crickets inside the skin of his buttocks and the backs of his thighs as he sits down. He feels their exoskeletons crunch and ooze beneath his weight. He wonders what will happen to their dead bodies now that they're trapped in there. Will they rot and fill with bacteria or will his body absorb them? He's not sure.

All of his punishments have been horrible but this one might be the worst. It is permanent torture and discomfort. Even his slug fingers seem pleasant in comparison. As he sits at his desk, he wiggles and squirms, trying to get comfortable, but the crickets keep moving. They crawl up his throat and burrow into his sinus cavities. He can feel them behind his eyeballs, scratching their prickly legs against the surface of his brain. It's the worst sensation he's ever experienced, worse than breaking his wrist when he fell off the monkey bars in the third grade. And every second he sits there, it feels like more and more of them are inside of him, like they are rapidly multiplying with every breath he takes.

It is absolute hell.

"Besides Benjamin, there is one more person who has failed their math test," says Mrs. Gustafson.

The children all freeze. They look at each other. It's been a long time since somebody else has failed a test in Mrs. Gustafson's class besides Benny. The only other person was a boy named Nick who was punished with severe acne that covered every centimeter of skin from head to toe, massive pus-filled zits like boils that made him look like he had leprosy or the plague. He was so embarrassed about it that he dropped Mrs. Gustafson's class and is now being homeschooled away from other kids. That's what Benny wishes he could have done if his parents didn't force him to stay in public school and deal with his punishments like a mature young man.

The school children wonder who the other failure could be. Many of the smart kids look around the room with big smiles on their faces, excited to see who the next kid they'll get to bully will be. Many of the not-so-smart kids cower in their seats with looks of terror in their eyes, praying that they are not the ones to fail.

Mrs. Gustafson looks at the girl with short black hair and blue frilly shirt that sits next to Benny.

"Mika, come up and take your punishment," the teacher says.

Mika jumps up with shock. "What? Me?"

"Yeah, you."

Everyone is surprised. Mika has always been a smart girl who always got good grades. Not good enough to receive prizes from the good box, but she always gets As and Bs, she's always on the honor roll.

"How the heck could I have failed?" she cries. "I should have aced that test!"

Mrs. Gustafson frowns at her. "You didn't fail because your answers were incorrect. You failed because you cheated. If you're caught cheating in my class, you get an instant F."

"I didn't cheat!" Mika screams. "I never cheat!"

Mrs. Gustafson shakes her head. "You were caught cheating. Amanda told me after class yesterday that you were copying her answers during the test."

"Amanda?" Mika looks at the blond girl sitting next her. "She's lying! She's just mad that I kissed her boyfriend on the bus last week!"

Amanda flashes a smug smile her way.

But the teacher doesn't believe her. "Don't try to deny it, Mika. Your test answers were identical to Amanda's. Now come up and accept your punishment like a good little girl."

Amanda begins snickering at her ex-friend and holds her hand up to her mouth so nobody can see.

"Fuck that!" Mika cries, standing up out of her seat. "This is bullshit! I didn't do anything!"

"Watch your language, young lady, and put your hand in the bad box."

"I'm not doing that!" Mika screams. "I'm going home!"

Mika turns and walks toward the door.

"Get back here, young lady! Do you want detention for a month?"

"You can expel me for all I care!"

But there's no escape from Mrs. Gustafson's classroom. Before Mika can reach the exit, the teacher's eyes grow red and a serpent of black smoke coils around her left arm, billowing up out of her skin. The door slams shut, right in Mika's face. Then the snake of black smoke shoots from the teacher's fingertips and wraps Mika up, dragging her kicking and screaming to the front of the room.

That's why Benny has always been terrified of Mrs. Gustafson. It's why he's never resisted accepting his punishments. As the person who invented the good box and the bad box, she has powers like no other teacher in the school. She is some kind of dark god from a dark dimension that you should never even think of crossing. The punishments from the black box pale in comparison to what she'll do to you if you really make her angry.

Mika struggles within the grips of the teacher's black powers. She cries, "I didn't cheat! I didn't cheat! Please, Mrs. Gustafson! You have to believe me!"

Amanda can't help but burst into laughter at her ex-friend's torment, sitting on the edge of her seat, waiting to see what will happen to her.

"Now take your punishment," says the teacher.

The black smoke pulls Mika's hand into the air and forces it down into the depths of the black box.

The girl continues to resist and scream, tears pouring from her eyes. "No! I don't want to!"

Once her hand is fully inside, a dark curse zaps into her soul. Her screams go silent. Her face stretches in horror. Then her body transforms into a ball of blue slime and splats on the floor.

She is no longer human. She has become a useless blob of goo, pulsing and bubbling beneath the teacher's feet. The other kids stare in horror. They've never seen such an awful punishment from the black box. Even Benny feels sorry for her. All fifteen of his punishments, even the slug fingers and crickets under his skin, are better than this.

Amanda breaks the silence by pointing and laughing. "Oh my god! She's become the blob! Mika's the blob now! Look at how gross she is!"

A mouth forms on the top of the blue blob and says, "What the hell is this shit!"

The teacher scolds her, "Language, young lady!"

Mika cries, "I'm a blob! How am I going to live as a blob?"

"You should have thought about that before you decided to cheat," says the teacher.

Mika's clothes have sunk into her translucent blue flesh and are beginning to dissolve.

"This is so unfair!" Mika says.

But Mrs. Gustafson doesn't respond to her. She puts the black box back into her desk and then goes to the whiteboard to begin her next lesson.

Mika oozes her way down the aisle to her desk next to Benny. All the kids stare at her, wondering how she's even able to see now that she doesn't have any eyes. Benny watches her as she tries to get into her chair, stretching out into a wave of slime that completely crashes against the seat and makes an audible splatting noise. The clothes inside of her body have almost completely dissolved already, leaving just a swirl of thread and her two faux-leather shoes.

Once Mika figures out how to pull her blobby form into the seat, Amanda leans in and whispers, "That's what you get for kissing Daniel, bitch."

The only people who hear are Mika, Benny and Tracy.

Even though she's all the way across the room, Tracy can hear everything with her gift of super hearing. She squints her eyes at Amanda and gives her a dirty look, even though nobody but Benny notices. Tracy appears to be just as angry about what she did as Mika. Benny wonders if she plans to tell the teacher about what she heard.

Mika oozes in the direction of her ex-friend and says, "You're so dead, Amanda. If I'm stuck like this for the rest of my life, trust me, I don't care what happens, you are fucking dead."

She doesn't bother whispering as she says this. Mika doesn't give a crap who hears her.

CHAPTER
TWO

At lunchtime, Benny sits alone at a dark table in the far corner of the cafeteria. It's pizza day which would have really cheered him up if it wasn't for his condition. He used to love eating pizza, but now that he has slugs for fingers he refuses to eat anything with his hands. The slugs leave a trail of wet mucus that have a terrible taste. Pizza, sandwiches, burgers—he can't eat any of that without a fork and knife. But, at school, he's only allowed plastic forks and knives and he always has a difficult time gripping them with his banana slug fingers.

It also doesn't help now that he has the cricket problem. While trying to take mangled bites of pizza, he can feel insects crawling up the back of his throat. He has to constantly swallow to keep them down. And when he finally gets a bite of food in his mouth, all he can taste are dead crickets. It's like they are dropping down from his nasal cavity into his mouth and getting chewed up between his teeth as he eats. He's worried that everything he eats from now on will be absolutely disgusting.

Across the lunch room, Heidi is shooting rainbows

from her hands as everyone applauds her. She has been welcomed at the popular girls' table, become one of the children blessed by the good box, and now she's happier than anyone has ever seen her. It's like she's won the lottery. It's better than Christmas and Easter and her birthday combined. And it's the same for Adam, welcomed at the popular boys' table, talking to all of them in Cantonese just to show off his new skill, despite it still not being that impressive to the rest of them.

Benny just looks down at his slug fingers and mangled pizza. He lets out a loud sigh, wishing that he could be like the smart popular kids. He wishes that he was one of them. He wishes he had taken gifts from the good box rather than punishments from the bad one. Even being a normal kid seems like an impossible dream now.

"Can I sit with you?" a voice comes from behind Benny.

He almost jumps from his seat. Nobody has ever spoken to him at lunch before. He turns to see the blue blob girl behind him, oozing and pulsing, holding up her food tray with two protruding limbs of slime.

Mika doesn't wait for Benny's response. She just splats into the chair next to him. "None of my friends will talk to me anymore."

Benny watches the mouth move on the side of her gelatinous form as she speaks, but he has no idea where her voice is coming from. She no longer has a throat or lungs or voice box. He just nods his head, not sure what to say.

"Look at those bitches," Mika says, nodding toward

a table of girls. It's the table where Amanda is sitting. The same table Mika used to sit. "They think they're so cool just because they're not blobs. They're nothing special. They don't even have super powers."

Mika groans, spraying a glob of goo against the side of Benny's neck.

"This sucks…" she says. "I was so close to getting an A+ on a test, I just know it. Now look at me. Even if I get a perfect score next time I'll still be stuck a stupid blob."

"That's not true." The goo on Benny's neck begins to burn. He swipes at it and brushes it off, tossing it back into Mika's body.

Mika looks at him with her eyeless form. "Yeah?"

"Mrs. Gustafson says if you get an A+ you can choose between a reward from the good box or having a punishment removed from the bad box. That's what she told me after class the first time I failed."

Mika swells with hope. "Well, that's what I'm going to have to do then, I guess. I'm not going to let Amanda get away with doing this to me. I can't believe she'd hold a grudge against me just because I kissed her stupid boyfriend. He doesn't even like her anymore anyway."

"So that's really what happened?" Benny asks. "You didn't really cheat?"

"Of course I didn't!" the blob girl stretches out with anger, becoming spiky and ruffled. "She cheated off of me! She's the one who should have gotten the bad box for cheating!"

Benny looks away from her and doesn't say anything else, not wanting to upset her further. She's always been

31

the most hotheaded kid in class. Benny thought she was scary even before she became a blob, but now she's even more intimidating than ever.

Mika looks down at her lunch tray. "How am I even supposed to eat like this?"

Benny shrugs.

Mika lifts the rectangle of pizza up with a fingerless limb of slime, the pizza sinking partially inside. Then she widens her giant mouth and drops her lunch inside. Benny can see the piece of pizza through her blue flesh as it sinks to the center of her body. He watches as it slowly dissolves inside of her next to the remains of her shoes and belt.

"Well, I guess I'm done eating already," Mika says. "I didn't taste a thing."

She turns to Benny and widens her mouth hole at him, pointing at the gooey depths within. "No taste buds."

Benny just shrugs and spits a cricket into his tray. The two of them watch it as it hops across the table to escape.

At recess, Mika follows Benny around the playground as though she has nothing better to do. Sand sticks to her gelatinous flesh, adhering to the bottom of her body like it would wet feet. She doesn't know how to get it off of her.

"So what do freaks do at recess anyway?" Mika asks.

Benny frowns. He points at the popular kids. "They

force us to be villains."

"Villains?"

Mika looks at the popular kids playing on the other side of the playground. They are playing superheroes. Since all the popular kids have received what they believe to be super powers from the good box, they have started to call themselves the Hero Squad. And their job is to defeat the super villains, the kids who draw from the bad box, which is normally just Benny.

"There they are!" Matty calls out from across the school yard, speaking in a proud superhero tone of voice. "The dastardly duo: Slug Hands and the other one…"

"She Blob!" Billy cries, as the team of superheroes rush toward the two freaks. "Let's call her She Blob!"

Matty agrees, "Yes, She Blob! Let us put an end to their evildoing!"

"And he's not Slug Hands anymore," Billy adds. "He's Cricket Boy. Call him Cricket Boy."

"Yes, Cricket Boy," Matty nods. "He is plotting to destroy the city with the power of his crickets!"

When the good guys confront Mika and Benny, Billy turns to his friends, "Who has the bravery to face them first?"

The new popular girl, Heidi, steps forward.

"I will!" she says in a cheerful tone. "My name is Rainbow Pixie and with the power of my rainbow blasts I will transform them with love into good guys who will only do good from this day forward!"

Then she shoots rainbows from her fingers into Benny's heart.

Billy looks at Heidi with irritation and shakes his head. He breaks character to say, "No, we don't want them to be good. They're the bad guys. We have to defeat them in combat."

"Then I will defeat them with love!" Heidi says.

Matty shakes his head, "New girl, you have to do it right or you're not allowed to play with us anymore."

Heidi frowns and backs away.

Adam steps forward and says, "Then I will face them." He points at his chest. "I'm Cantonese Man! I'll speak Cantonese at them so fast that they'll get dizzy and confused! Then the rest of you can go in and finish them off!"

Billy shrugs. "Sure… I guess that'll work."

He nods at the rest of the super team. They all get prepared. Black Thunder opens his mouth, getting ready to yell so loud that everyone in the county can hear him. The Poison Arrow gets ready to shoot them with invisible deadly darts, even though his power is just that he's immune to all poisons and doesn't actually have the power to poison anyone. And Rock Girl squeezes her fists and gets ready to clobber them with the strength of ten gorillas.

"Okay, ready team?" Billy shouts. "Go!"

Adam steps forward and speaks in Cantonese, "Wǒmen huì zǔzhǐ nǐ de xié'è zhī lù!"

Benny plays along. He pretends to be confused and stunned by Adam's super power. He knows that it's a good idea to play along. If he doesn't then they'll really get nasty with him.

But Mika isn't having any of it. The blob girl just looks at Benny, then at Adam. Then she says, "You douchebags better just back off!"

The super kids break character. They freeze in their place, intimidated just by the girl's voice.

"You want to start shit?" she says, oozing toward them. "I'll destroy all of you motherfuckers!"

The super kids are shocked by her words. They've never heard a kid swear so much in school before, not even on the playground. But Mika just doesn't give a shit anymore. Getting in trouble doesn't mean anything once you've already received the worst punishment you're ever going to get.

Adam immediately apologizes and backs away, hiding behind the other kids. But Billy and Matty aren't as easily intimidated by the slime girl's words. Even though they are shaking a little, they return to character and step toward her.

"You are no match for us, She Blob!" Billy says.

Mika bounces at him. "Don't call me She Blob, Four Eyes!"

Billy opens his mouth to yell back at her, but doesn't know what to say.

She turns to Matty. "You, too, Matty the Fatty. Think you're cool just because you can breathe underwater? I'll destroy you."

Matty looks down at his pudgy gut and frowns. "I'm not that fat…"

"I'll destroy all you dorks!"

Billy gets angry. He's never had a super villain yell

at him this much before.

"Don't be afraid, Hero Squad!" he tells his friends. "I'll vanquish this foe with my super stretchy powers!"

Billy makes a fist and spins it like a helicopter around his head, preparing to give her a super punch. His arm moves like it's made of rubber, stretching to three times its natural length.

But before he can do anything, Mika widens her massive gooey mouth and swallows Billy whole. Everyone can see him floating inside her gelatinous body, thrashing and trying to escape. The kids stare at him in horror.

"Spit him out!" Heidi cries. "He can't breathe!"

Mika just gives her a blobby shrug. "Can't. Don't know how."

Billy chokes and gags inside of her, his screams muffled, his clothes beginning to melt.

Mika steps toward the other superheroes. "Anybody else want to be eaten?"

The heroes back away from her, all of them but Matty. He says, "You can't eat me, villain! I'm Ghost Man!"

Matty uses his power of passing through solid objects to save his friend. He enters her body, grabs Billy and tries to pull him out. But in order to grab his friend he has to release his ghost powers, which will leave his arm vulnerable. He gives it a try anyhow, but takes only three tugs before he gives up and lets go.

The pudgy kid rubs his arm and says, "Ow, that burns!" Then he runs away with the others to regroup.

Benny looks at the kid dissolving inside of Mika. Billy reaches out to him, begging to be saved. He's never looked so helpless and pathetic. His glasses are floating in the slime next to him, the plastic frame becoming warped in the goo. His eyes roll back. The lack of oxygen is stealing his consciousness. If Mika doesn't spit him out he's going to die soon.

Mika tries puking but the kid doesn't come out.

"Shit…" she says. "I think he's really stuck in me…"

She looks up at Benny with ruffled flesh, becoming anxious. "What do I do? I don't actually want to kill him."

Benny looks around. He's not sure.

Mika cries, "I don't want to end up digesting him. That will be gross!"

When Benny turns to look for help, he sees the superheroes coming back at them. They are all charging, ready to attack. But they aren't playing anymore. This time they're serious. They're going to beat Benny and Mika to death if they don't figure out how to free their friend immediately.

A flash of light passes between them. It swoops down from the clouds and rips Billy out of Mika's guts. Blue slime splashes across the sand, spraying all the kids on the merry-go-round. When Benny looks back, he sees Tracy hovering in the air above them. She holds the soaking wet Billy in her arms, her angel wings flapping majestically. The sun behind her head looks like a halo of light.

Tracy goes by *Cupid* on the playground. She is the leader of the Hero Squad. Even though she spends most of recess flying through the clouds like a mighty white eagle, completely forgetting about the miserable world below, she sometimes comes down to help the other super kids or give them missions or chores to do for her. It makes them happy and often keeps them out of trouble.

Billy coughs up blue slime and gasps for air. Then she lowers him to his feet where he collapses into the sand and catches his breath.

Mika oozes back together. Having Billy ripped out of her body tore apart her gelatinous form, spreading her into several wet chunks. Once she becomes a single mass again, she says, "Why did she have to be so rough? That kind of hurt."

"Cupid!" the superhero team cries. "Cupid's here! She saved Billy! Cupid is the best!"

They point at Benny and Mika. "Defeat the supervillains for us! Beat them up for what they did to our ally!"

Cupid lets out a sigh, not really wanting to be bothered by all this nonsense. "Very well, I'll stop these villains for their wrongdoings once and for all."

The super kids cheer for her, raising their fists and jumping up and down.

Tracy turns to Benny and Mika, pretending to act serious. She lands on the ground and uses her growing power to become a giantess, expanding her form until she is a hundred feet tall. The other superheroes cheer her on as she reaches down and picks up the super villains, one in each hand.

She looks at Mika in her left hand and says in a mock superhero voice, albeit an overly bored one, "You'll never eat my teammates again, She Blob."

Then she flicks Mika across the yard like a big blue

38

booger. The blob girl screams as she soars through the air and splats against the wall of the gymnasium. She leaves a trail of blue ooze as she slides down to the sidewalk, but doesn't seem to be damaged in any way.

"Now you, Cricket Boy," Cupid says, turning her attention to the final villain.

When he looks in her eyes, Benny can't help but blush. It all happened so fast that he's only now just realizing what's happening to him. The most beautiful girl in school is holding him in the palm of her hand, handling him like a doll, staring down on him with her wide glossy eyes. He can feel the warmth of her big white fingers curled around him. He can feel her fingerprints against his forearms, her sweat moistening his shirt and pants. He can even feel her hot breaths as she brings him closer to her face. Even though it's frightening to be so high in the air, he can't help but feel protected by her. She is not a bully like the rest of them. She is a kindhearted goddess who loves and protects everyone. She is the only person in their class who is a *real* superhero.

"This is going to hurt a little," she whispers to him, though even a whisper is a booming voice for his miniature size. "Just play along and I'll make sure they leave you alone afterward."

Benny nods his head and smiles, but then feels the wind knocked from his lungs as Tracy squeezes her fingers around him.

"Take this, Cricket Boy," Tracy shouts so loud that everyone on the playground can hear her. "I'll squish you like the little bug that you are!"

Benny squeals as the giant angel turns her hand into a fist, squeezing the life out of him. Even though it's all just for show, it doesn't exactly feel like Tracy is pretending. His arms and legs fold in unnatural directions, dangling between her fingers. His stomach is compressed so much that he pukes crickets out of his nose and mouth. He's not quite sure if the girl is actually trying to crush him or just doesn't yet understand her own strength when she's in giant form.

"Squish! Squish! Squish!" Tracy yells.

When Tracy winks at him, Benny lets out a fake death rattle and then pretends to go limp. The super kids all cheer with excitement.

"She did it!" they cry. "Cupid defeated the villains!"

The giant girl lowers Benny's body to the playground, but doesn't set him by her feet where the super kids are standing. She bends over the merry-go-round and the monkey bars and lays him close to Mika, away from kids who might want to bully him further.

Cupid returns to her normal size and lets all of the other kids praise her for saving the day. Then she leaps into the air and flies off.

When Mika oozes to Benny's side, both of them looking up at the clouds to watch Cupid fly away, she asks, "What the hell is that bitch's problem?"

"Tracy was just trying to save us," Benny says with a dumb smile on his face. "She's my hero."

Benny is still quivering with exhilaration from being held in his angel's hand. He feels as if he's been touched by a goddess. Even though he knows such a perfect being would never be interested in him, he still feels blessed to have been saved by her. He still feels special that she even cares enough to stop the others from bullying him.

Mika sighs at Benny when she sees him making lovey-dovey eyes at the clouds where Tracy is flying. She tries to get his mind off of the super girl.

"We need to make a plan," she says.

"A plan?"

The blob nods. "We need to ace the history test tomorrow so that we can get our curses removed."

Benny looks down.

"What?" she asks, oozing closer to him. "You don't think we can do it?"

"Maybe you can…"

"You can, too. I'll help you study."

"It won't work…"

"You're not even going to try? What's wrong with you? Do you want to be a dumb loser for the rest of your life?"

"I'm not dumb."

"You're acting dumb. You fail every test you take and don't even try."

"I try. I study harder than anyone."

"Then why do you always fail?"

"I know every answer on every test I've taken. I just

can't think straight. I'm always so scared that I'll fail that I just… I just freeze up."

Mika lets out a burst of laughter. "Is that all? You're just nervous?"

Benny nods his head. "I get good grades on everything else I do because there's no danger of getting the bad box with other assignments. It's just the tests that I fail."

She slaps him on the back with a limb of slime. "You just need confidence. I can help you with that."

"Really? You think I can change?"

"Of course you can. It's easy. You help me study and I'll help you become brave. Together we'll get a hundred percent on every test we take, remove our curses and then get more gifts from the good box than anyone else in class!"

Benny looks at her and smiles. He's never had anybody help him with anything before. Not even his parents.

"So we're a team?" Benny asks.

Mika nods. "We're not just a team…" She glares at the super kids across the playground. "We're a super villain team!"

Then she slaps him on the back and giggles with glee. Benny isn't convinced that they'll succeed, but he likes the girl's optimism.

On the way back to class, the newly formed super villain team passes Billy in the hallway. A crowd is standing around him, wondering what happened. His clothes are wet and full of holes. His skin is bright red, like he's received a horrible sunburn on his face and arms. Several layers of his skin have been melted off. He doesn't seem like he needs emergency medical attention, but he's definitely rattled by his experience on the playground.

He jumps at the sight of Mika as the freak kids pass him in the hall. Her blob mouth curls into a smug smile as she oozes by, telling him without words that he better not fuck with them again. Billy doesn't have to say anything. The look in his eyes shows that he'll never cross them another time, no matter what.

Amanda is among the students crowded around Billy. She looks at the boy's skin and back at Mika, an expression of panic spreads across her face.

Mika just says, "You're next, bitch," as she slides by, leaving a trail of blue slime behind her.

Amanda backs away and doesn't say a thing. It's just finally dawning on her how much she fucked up. Her ex-friend might have drawn a punishment from the bad box, but the power she obtained is not something to be messed around with. Mika has become one of the deadliest kids in the class.

"We'll show her," Mika whispers to Benny. "We'll show them all."

CHAPTER
THREE

After school, Mika comes over to Benny's house to study. When she shows up at the front door, his parents freak out. They don't even know that Mika is a human girl. At first, they think some neighborhood kids dropped off a huge pile of steaming blue toxic waste on their doorstep as some kind of practical joke, but once the goo starts talking to them they recoil in disgust.

Benny's parents aren't fans of freakish human beings like Mika. They don't even like the kids who have received gifts from the good box, like Tracy and Heidi. They think they all are a bunch of horrific monsters that should be avoided as much as possible. That's why Benny no longer lives in the main house with the rest of the family. They have him living in the pool house in the backyard where they don't have to look at him anymore. He hasn't even spoken to his family in person for months.

"Seriously?" Mika says when she enters Benny's pool house. "They force you to live out here?"

Benny shrugs. "It's not so bad. I have my own television and my own refrigerator and microwave and air conditioning." He points at everything in the pool house. It actually is pretty nice. Like a one bedroom apartment, but decorated for a kid with video games and movie posters and action figure displays. "I'm just not allowed to go in the house anymore."

He tries to show his enthusiasm for his current situation, but it's obvious that he feels terrible about being rejected by his family. It's obvious that they don't love him as much as normal parents would love their child. It's also pretty obvious that they treated him this way long before he first put his hand inside of the bad box.

"My mom is the opposite," Mika says, oozing into the center of the living room section of his pool house. "When she sees me like this she'll probably give me twenty banana splits and buy me a million toys and won't leave me alone for a second until I freak out on her. She's so annoying like that."

Benny nods his head, but really has no idea what that would be like. His parents have always treated him more like an obligation than anything. He couldn't imagine them buying him toys and treats whenever something bad happened to him at school.

"Check this out," Mika tells Benny.

When he looks in her direction, she protrudes a blue limb from her ball of slime and then extends five fingers from the tip of it, loosely resembling a hand.

"What is it?" Benny asks.

Mika rumbles with annoyance. "What do you mean *what is it?* Do you know how hard it is to do stuff with this body? I'm trying to make a hand."

Benny nods. "It looks kind of like a hand."

"And look at this," she says.

Mika lifts her blobby form off of the ground and creates two long limbs from the bottom of the mass, somewhat resembling human legs.

"Legs?" Benny asks. "Can you walk on them?"

"Not yet." Mika takes a step and her whole body splats on the floor. "I can hardly hold the shape for more than a few seconds. But I think I can if I keep practicing."

Benny nods. "That would be cool."

"Even if I'm stuck as a blob I want to be able to do all the stuff I used to be able to do. I want to dance and ride a bike and play volleyball and draw pictures. There's no way I'm going to let this curse ruin my life."

Benny smiles. He's never met anyone like Mika before. All year, Benny's curses have only been things he regrets and endures and tries to ignore. He never had the courage to try to accept his defects and find a way to overcome them.

"You better not let your curses ruin your life, either," Mika tells him. "There's no quitters allowed on our super villain team."

Benny nods his head and opens his mouth to speak, but instead of words he only releases a family of chirping crickets across the pool house floor.

Mika practices forming a human hand from her blobby mass as she lifts flash cards from a pile on the floor and reads off questions to Benny.

"What date did Robert E. Lee surrender to Ulysses S. Grant?" she asks him, trying to hold the card steady.

"April 9th, 1865," Benny responds.

Mika looks at the answer. "Yep." She lifts the next card. "How many soldiers died during the Civil War?"

"620,000," answers Benny.

Mika nods and lifts the next flash card, trying to balance it between two blue tendril fingers.

"Who ran in the election of 1860?"

Benny looks up at the ceiling, thinking for a few seconds, and then responds, "Lincoln, Douglas, Breckenridge, and Bell."

"These questions are hard," Mika says. "I can't believe you know all of this."

She asks five more questions and Benny answers all five of them correctly.

"You really are smart," she says.

Benny takes the flash cards from Mika's goo hands and shuffles them. "I told you I study harder than everyone in the class."

"So it really is just nervousness?"

Benny nods. "My mind goes blank when I'm nervous."

"Then what you need to do is practice answering questions when you're nervous."

"How do I do that?"

"How about you run down the street naked as I quiz you?"

Benny furiously shakes his head. "No way! I'm not doing that! If I get caught my parents will kill me."

"What if we went to the top of a tall building and dangled you off the edge?"

This freaks Benny out even more. "Are you crazy? That's too dangerous!"

"So is failing another test."

"It's not going to work. It would take weeks or months of trying to answer questions under pressure before I'd get over my fear. The test is tomorrow. I need something easier."

Mika thinks about it for a minute. She makes a hand out of slime and rubs a section of her formless body that resembles a chin.

"Oh, I know..." she says, pointing up at the ceiling with a blue finger. "You just need to learn some relaxation techniques. My mom is into yoga and knows all about releasing tension."

Benny's expression becomes more hopeful. "Really?"

Mika nods. "I'll teach you breathing exercises and how to clear your mind. Just focusing on how you breathe will do a lot to calm your anxiety."

Benny wonders if it could be that simple. "I normally breathe really fast when I take a test. When I really panic I sometimes don't even breathe at all."

"Deep breaths," Mika says, opening her wide maw and imitating the act of deep breathing, even though she no longer needs to breathe like a human. "Take slow deep breaths."

Benny gives it a shot but is too busy smiling to do it properly. He can't believe he never tried something so simple before. If he can calm down he knows he'll ace the test for sure.

Mika uses her tendrils to collect all the laminated flash cards into a pile and says, "So you teach me everything you know about the Civil War and I'll teach you everything I know about releasing stress."

Benny nods with excitement. "Yeah. We'll ace the test tomorrow for sure!"

Mika grins. "That's the spirit." She forms a hand with her goo and raises it up to Benny. "Go team super villains!"

Benny gives her a high five so hard that blue slime sprays across the room and all over his comic book collection. He doesn't realize the goo is melting the latest issue of X-Men as they get deep into study mode.

After a long night of studying and memorizing and meditating and eating Hot Pockets, the two freak kids feel more prepared for the test than any test they've ever taken in their lives.

As Mrs. Gustafson passes out the history test, Benny focuses on the stress release techniques that Mika taught him. He closes his eyes and presses his index finger into the center of his palm. Then he breathes in deeply for a count of three, then breathes out. As he exhales, he clears his mind and thinks of the color blue. Blue is his favorite color and the color that relaxes him most, so he imagines a world where everything is blue.

When he opens his eyes, he continues to take deep breaths and imagines the entire classroom is the color blue. The other students are able to start the test ten minutes before him so he's able to spend extra time on the meditation exercise. He looks over at Mika, who also has to wait ten minutes before starting. She gives him a blobby smile and a thumbs up.

Benny doesn't smile back, too focused on his breathing. He tries not to think of anything. Just the color blue. For a moment, he starts to think about how unfair it is that kids who fail have ten minutes less time than everyone else. Once a student starts failing, it becomes harder and harder for them to obtain a passing grade. It makes Benny so angry that his breaths quicken and the color of the room goes from blue to purple. But he quickly catches himself and clears his mind and goes back to taking deep breaths.

When ten minutes have passed, Mrs. Gustafson puts the test in front of the two failing students. Benny imagines that the paper in front of him is a light shade of blue instead of white. He can see the questions clearly for the first time this year. He already knows the answers to the first five questions before he even picks up his pencil. This is what he's been waiting for. He realizes he can do this now. He can really pass this test. Maybe he can even get a perfect score.

Benny decides to take one last deep breath before

starting. As he inhales, a cricket crawling up his throat gets swept up in his breath. It becomes lodged in his breathing passageway. His heart races as he realizes he can't breathe, choking on a stupid cricket. His face turns red. The questions on his test go blurry.

He looks at Mika for help, but she's having problems of her own. She's unable to hold up her pencil in her goo hand. No matter how many fingers she creates, the pencil just won't stay steady enough to write. It falls to her desk every time she presses it to the paper and gets stuck inside of her slime whenever she tries to pick it up.

"Stupid blob hands!" Mika cries.

The teacher shushes her.

Realizing Mika won't be any help to him, Benny stands up, looking at the teacher, making gagging noises as a way to signal he's in trouble.

But Mrs. Gustafson just says, "Stay in your seat, Benjamin."

He points at his throat, trying to explain that he's choking. But the teacher doesn't seem to care. The other kids are so focused on their test that they don't even seem to notice his emergency.

"I said sit down," says the teacher.

Benny lowers himself into his chair and tries massaging his throat, tries coughing the cricket up, he even tries giving himself the Heimlich maneuver against the edge of his desk. But nothing works. The thing won't budge. He gets dizzy and his mind grows faint. He realizes there's a good chance that he might just choke to death right then and there.

"My test is melting!" Mika cries.

Benny looks over at her and sees the paper dissolving within her blob hand. It somehow got stuck inside of her slime and she can't get it out.

"It's ruined!" she cries. "I need a new test!"

But Mrs. Gustafson just shushes her again and says, "No talking during a test, young lady."

Mika cries and panics as the piece of paper fades away within her body. "This is so unfair!"

Benny can't worry about her, though. He's got his own problem to deal with. He feels like he's about to lose consciousness. He takes one last attempt to ram the top of his stomach against the edge of the desk, but it's no good. He collapses on top of his test and can no longer move. But just before his mind goes black, he feels the cricket struggling to get free. The second it squeezes its way out of his breathing passageway, Benny lets out such a powerful cough that it shoots the cricket across two desks and lands in Amanda's hair.

Taking long hard pants, Benny sits upright and calms himself. He's alive. That's all that matters right now. He didn't choke to death in the middle of class. But as he breathes, he feels a calmness coming over him. His mind clears. When he looks at the test, he realizes that the questions are in perfect focus.

Without thinking, he picks up his pencil and writes down the answer to the first question. Then he writes the second one. Then the third. He doesn't worry about whether he passes or fails the test. He just takes it one question at a time. And before he knows it, he's answered the final question. The test is completely filled out and there's not a single answer that he doesn't feel completely confident about.

This is it, he thinks to himself. *I've finally done it. I've finally passed a test.* Then he pauses for a moment. *No, I didn't just pass it. I'm going to get a hundred. I'm going to get something from the good box!*

A big smile spreads across his face as he passes it to the front of the class. He feels bad for Mika, who wasn't able to answer a single question, but he knows at least he did well. He can finally prove to everyone that he's not the dumbest kid in class. If he does this every time, he can finally remove all of his curses and be a regular kid again. Maybe he can even be a super kid.

Benny spends the rest of the day in a state of euphoria. He can't even remove the stupid smile from his face as he tries to console Mika at lunchtime. It's all just too much for him. He's not a test-failer anymore. He's a test-passer. A perfect scorer. A winner. And someday everyone will finally like him again. Even Tracy. Even Billy and the other boys. Even his parents.

CHAPTER
FOUR

For the first time all school year, Benny can't wait to hear the test results. Instead of trembling in horror as he usually does, he now sits straight up with his hands folded on his desk, smiling cheerfully. He can't wait for the teacher to read off the students who did best on the history test.

Mrs. Gustafson pulls out the good box and places it on the table. Benny breathes in its heavenly aura. He's finally going to be able to go to it, to put his hand inside like all the popular kids always get to do. But now he has to decide whether to remove one of his curses or obtain one of the rewards. He knows he should just remove a curse. He would especially like to remove the crickets from his body. Yesterday, that curse almost killed him. But there's a part of him that wants to gain something from the good box. Something useful. Something that will make him special. What's the use of removing one curse when he'll still have fourteen left? He might even get a really good reward like curse-removal that will let him remove all of his defects in one go and prevent him from ever getting another one again. He could even remove Mika's curse or any curse that any kid gets from the bad box ever again. He knows the chances of attaining such a gift are next to impossible, but he likes to dream that such a gift could be obtainable. He likes to think that all of his problems could be solved with just one touch of the good box.

"Three students excelled at yesterday's history test," says Mrs. Gustafson. "All three received a score of 100 percent. You should all be proud to share a class with such shining intellects."

Benny did it. He's sure he scored a hundred. He can't wait to hear his name called.

"The first to receive a reward from the good box is, as you might have guessed, Tracy Wilson."

The crowd cheers for her. "Go Cupid! You're the best!"

Tracy glides to the front of the room like a swan and accepts yet another prize. This time she receives the ability to read minds.

"Congratulations, Tracy," the teacher says.

The class applauds as the angel returns to her seat.

Benny is so focused on winning his own prize that the reality of Tracy's gift doesn't hit him quite yet. But once he thinks about it for a moment, he begins to panic. If Tracy has the power to read minds then she'll be able to read his mind. She'll learn about how much he's in love with her. She'll know that he thinks about her all the time, during class, during recess. It'll make her hate him. She'll think it will be gross and horrible that he has a crush on her. It will be so embarrassing that he'll want to die.

As the teacher reads off the next name, Benny tries not to think about the girl he has a crush on. He tries not to look over at her, not even at her beautiful white hair or white angel wings. He needs to pretend that she doesn't even exist. So he focuses on the teacher. He can't let his mind wander.

"Andrea Lovett," the teacher calls out.

Andrea, or *Rock Girl* as she's called on the playground, goes up to receive her reward. She gets the power to control how she smells. Although not that impressive of a gift, Benny would love to receive that ability. He's cursed with rotten egg stench, not to mention slug and dead cricket smells, so he'd love the ability to smell like roses. He could even make his farts smell like cotton candy if he wanted them to.

"And the final student to receive a reward from the good box…" Mrs. Gustafson begins.

The children move to the edges of their seats with anticipation. Many of them think it might be them who got a perfect score. But they're wrong. Benny knows whose name will be called. It's going to be him. He's certain of it. There's no way he got a single question wrong. Once Mrs. Gustafson reads Benny's name, all the other kids are going to freak out. Benny just knows it will be the shock of the school year. The day Benny Paulson scored 100 on a test. It's his golden moment and he plans to relish every moment of it.

As the name is called, Benny gets up from his seat, ready to accept his reward. But it's not his name that is spoken.

His jaw goes slack when the teacher says, "Amanda Knight."

Everyone but Benny and Mika applaud her. It's impossible. Benny knows he should have scored a hundred and there's no way Amanda could score that high. She's never been a failure like Benny, but she's definitely not an honor student. She has a C minus average in all her subjects. There's no way she could have gotten a hundred from studying. Since she sits next to Andrea, she must have cheated off of her just like she cheated off of Mika on the math test.

Amanda smirks at Mika as she puts her hand in the good box and receives her gift. All the students drop their jaws in amazement when she tells them her new ability. She has gained the power to breathe fire like a dragon. She opens her mouth and blows a ball of flames over the heads of Mika and Benny, just to show the class how great she is now. They all applaud with awe and delight. It is one of the most powerful and destructive gifts anyone has ever received.

When Amanda returns to her seat next to Mika, she leans in close to her ex-friend and whispers, "I wonder how fast slime burns."

But Mika doesn't have a comeback for her. She's too busy worrying about her punishment from the bad box to care about anything Amanda has to say. Since she accidentally melted her test yesterday and wasn't even able to turn it in, she knows her score is a big fat zero.

When Mika is finally called to accept another curse from the bad box, it turns out to not be all that bad this time. The curse is *frog tongue*.

All the kids point and laugh at the blob girl, but she shrugs it off right away. If she was still human having a frog tongue might have been mortifying, but now that she's a blob it's not really much of a curse. It might even be advantageous for eating popcorn or pizza rolls from a bowl.

Mika opens her maw and releases a long blue frog tongue, launching it in and out of her mouth for the rest of the class to see. They cringe and giggle and say, "Ewwwww!" but Mika doesn't care. She accepts her punishment and returns to her seat. Billy quivers in fear as she whips her tongue out one more time, right over his head, almost to tease him with it. She wanted to give him one more reason not to mess with her on the playground ever again.

Benny assumes that Mika is the only student to fail. Everyone else looks pretty confident in their scores, not a single one of them showing any sign of panic or worry. But there is one more person who failed. One more person who has to draw from the bad box.

Everyone is sure that it will be Benny. It's always Benny. But he knows for a fact that it won't be him. He did well. Very well. Maybe he didn't get a perfect score like he thought he did, but he's positive that he got at least a B+ or an A. He's definitely safe from the bad box.

But Mrs. Gustafson calls out his name anyway. "Benjamin, come up and accept your punishment."

Benny's mouth drops open in shock. He can't believe it. There's no way he failed. He did well this time. He really did well. There has to be some kind of mistake.

For the first time ever, Benny finds himself standing up for himself. He says, "I didn't fail, Mrs. Gustafson. I know I didn't."

All the kids laugh at him. Of course they think he failed. The idea that he could actually pass is ridiculous to them.

"I answered every question this time," he continues. "I'm sure I got almost all of them right."

Mrs. Gustafson shakes her head at him. "I know you got them all right, Benjamin. You got a perfect score. You got one hundred percent."

The children go quiet. They're confused by their teacher's words. Benny is especially perplexed.

"Then why do I have to accept a punishment from the bad box?" he asks.

The teacher rolls her eyes and explains, "Because you obviously cheated. There's no way that you could possibly have answered all the questions correctly. I would have bought it if you scored a sixty-one or even a seventy. But a hundred? It's impossible. You lack the intelligence to even cheat properly."

All the children burst into laughter. None of them, not the teacher or the students, consider that he could have possibly gotten a hundred percent on his own. They think he's too dumb. He's a loser. He can only do well if he cheats.

Benny can't believe it. He gets so flustered he can't think of anything else to say in his defense but, "I didn't cheat! I swear!"

This only makes the other children laugh harder.

"I don't want any backtalk, Benjamin," says the teacher. "Come get your punishment for being a dirty rotten cheater."

Benny doesn't know what to do. He looks at Mika, hoping that she'll back him up, but she just looks at him in her blobby form. Based on the bubbles growing on her back, he assumes she's just as mad and frustrated as he is. But there's nothing either of them can do about it. Mrs. Gustafson has all the power and if she says Benny cheated then Benny cheated. It's not like he can complain to the principal or his parents or anything.

The kids boo and laugh as Benny reluctantly staggers to the front of the class. He doesn't hesitate this time. He drops his hand directly into the bad box and takes his punishment.

This time he doesn't quite understand the curse he receives.

"What did you get this time?" the kids in the front row ask, giggling under their words.

He says, "Lightning magnetism? What's that mean?"

The second he asks this a bolt of lightning strikes through the ceiling and pierces right into the top of his head. A surge of energy pulses through his body and he drops to his knees. He can feel his skin sizzling and see smoke coming off of his clothes. He doesn't know how he's still alive.

The kids freeze in shock at the lightning strike, looking up at the burnt hole in the ceiling and then down at Benny's charred body. Then they explode into laughter.

Benny picks himself up and tries to balance himself as he walks back to his seat.

"Maybe everyone should move their chairs an extra six feet away from Benjamin," the teacher tells her students. "It might not be safe to be situated too close to his vicinity."

The teacher doesn't bother sending Benny to the nurse's office. He should probably go to the hospital. But Mrs. Gustafson just goes right back to her lesson, showing absolutely zero concern for a failing, cheating student.

As Benny sits there, still in a daze, smelling of burnt ham, he notices that he doesn't feel any crickets crawling under his skin anymore. He wonders if they were all electrocuted to death, their tiny corpses now just curled up husks buried somewhere inside of him. Even though he was accused of cheating and received another curse, at least one good thing has come of it.

But just as Benny tries to look on the bright side, he feels a whole new brood of crickets spawning in the center of his body.

At lunch, Mika is pissed. She eats her chicken nuggets with her gooey blue tongue and swallows them whole, cursing the teacher and Amanda and all the students.

"That was bullshit," she says. "You didn't cheat. Who

the hell could you have even cheated off of? The other students who scored that high sit on the other side of the room."

Benny nods. "Mrs. Gustafson hates me. That's what I think. She just hates me."

"What are we going to do?" Mika asks. "I can't take a test with this body. There's no way. And if Mrs. Gustafson always thinks you're cheating even when you do well, how are you supposed to pass a test? You'll never get rid of any curses."

The two outcast students frown at their lunch trays, wondering if their situation is hopeless. They see the popular kids welcoming Amanda into their fold. She accepts their friendship, quickly abandoning her old table of friends, and immediately proceeds to act like the queen bee of the girl's table, second only to Tracy. Although it's only her first time receiving a gift from the good box, she does have a frightening power and everyone is envious of her for having it. They all want her to join their superhero team and become their new best friend.

"That cheating bitch," Mika says, glaring at Amanda across the lunch room. "I can't believe she got away with it. She gets fire powers and I get turned into a blob? It's so not fair."

Benny agrees. Nothing about Mrs. Gustafson's class is fair. He wishes he would have gone to a different class, had a different teacher. He wishes he could just switch schools and never see those horrible boxes ever again.

"We're not going to get ahead if we play by the rules." Mika empties the rest of her food tray into her open maw. "We need a new plan."

Benny looks over at her. "Like what?"

"I think it's time we go into full-on super villain mode," she says.

Benny doesn't understand.

"I say we break into school at night and steal both the bad box and the good box. Then we can get rid of the curses ourselves. We can have all the powers we want."

Benny shivers at the idea. He's always thought about doing something like that. Stealing the boxes would be the answer to all of his problems. But he's never had the nerve. It seems too risky. Too dangerous.

"Are you serious?"

Mika slaps her blobby form with a blue limb. "Hell yeah, I'm serious. It's the only option we have left."

"What if we get caught?"

"Maybe we will but it's worth a shot. What else are we going to do?"

Benny thinks about it for a moment and then nods his head. "We'll have to come up with a good plan. I'm sure Mrs. Gustafson wouldn't make it easy to steal the boxes."

"I'm sure there's a way to succeed if we try hard enough. There's not another test for at least a month, so we have time to figure everything out."

Benny stares at his slug fingers, wondering if they can get away with it. He sure would love to get rid of all of his terrible curses. He would love to never have to pull another punishment from the bad box ever again.

"Do you think we'll really get away with it?" Benny asks.

Mika nods her head. "Though if we do it, we'll never be able to come back to school ever again. We might have to run away from home and go far away, somewhere Mrs. Gustafson will never find us."

Benny frowns and lowers his eyes. The idea of running away from home doesn't sit well with him.

"You don't have a problem with that, do you?" Mika asks. "I saw your living situation. Your family has already disowned you anyway."

"Yeah, but where will we go? What will we do for money?"

Mika laughs. "We'll have the good box, dummy. We'll have so many powers that we'll be able to do anything we want. We can rob banks if we have to. Maybe we'll even get the power to turn anything into money, like Tracy. Nobody will be able to stop us."

"We'll live like super villains?" Benny asks.

"Exactly!" Mika cries. "Now you get it!"

Then Mika lets out a deep and menacing laugh as though imitating the laugh of a cliché super villain. She keeps doing the menacing laugh until Benny finally joins her and they chuckle sinisterly in unison. They don't stop, even after the other kids in the cafeteria start staring at them and calling them weird.

CHAPTER
FIVE

For the next two weeks, Mika and Benny get together during lunch and after school every day for their super villain team meetings. They work on strategies for how they can break into the school and steal Mrs. Gustafson's magic boxes. The first and most crucial obstacle is how they can get through the school's locked doors. There are three doors they'll have to get through—the side entrance, the entrance to the fifth grade wing, and the door to their classroom. Mika will be the one to accomplish this for them. She has been practicing the art of squeezing her body flat and oozing through cracks under doors. She's gotten so good at it that she can even squeeze through keyholes if she needed to. If she can get to the other side of the door it will be easy to unlock it and let Benny through. She might even be able to unlock the door as she passes through the keyhole if she practices enough.

Benny, on the other hand, is responsible for cracking the combination safe in Mrs. Gustafson's desk where the boxes are kept. His slug fingers might be messy and slimy and make it difficult to do things that normal fingers can do, but they work very well when it comes to certain things. The slugs can sense even the slightest vibrations, so Benny doesn't need any other special safe-cracking equipment. He can easily sense the tiny clicking sound while turning a combination lock with his slug fingers.

On the playground at recess, Mika times Benny as he tries to crack ten combination locks in a row. Mika has gotten so adept at forming human-shaped blob arms that she can now hold a stopwatch with ease.

"Sixty-eight seconds," Mika says as Benny finishes opening the last lock. "That's a new record."

Benny exhales a cricket and says, "I still want to be able to do it in under a minute. Let's keep going."

Mika shakes her head. "Let's take a break. Sixty-eight seconds is more than enough time. You only need to crack one lock. You'll be able to do it in less than ten seconds. It will be easy!"

Benny sits back in the sand and puts his hands in his lap. "I'm just worried that I might freeze up when the time comes. I can't do anything when I'm nervous."

Mika wraps her blue arm around Benny's shoulders. "Don't worry about it. You can just do the breathing exercises I taught you. It'll be a piece of cake."

Benny nods. He wants to believe her, but it's difficult for him to not worry about it. Worrying about everything has always been in his nature.

Mika stands up and brushes the sand off of her body. She's been getting good at taking human shape lately. Although her head is just a smooth blue ball and her legs don't have any feet, she's still able to come across as somewhat human now. She doesn't have to be stuck in blob form all the time. She kind of reminds Benny of a living stick figure drawn with blue paint.

"I think we're ready," Mika says.

"Ready for what?"

"The heist of course," she says, pointing at the school building. "We just need to pick a date."

"I don't know if we're ready yet. There's still so much to consider…"

"We're not going to get any more ready than this. All we need to do is pack our stuff so that we can run away immediately after the deed is done. We could probably go as soon as tomorrow night if we wanted to."

"So soon?" There's a nervous tone in Benny's voice.

"Yeah, let's just go for it."

Benny looks away from her, wondering if they should really go through with the mission. If they fail they'll be in more trouble than they've ever been in their lives. Benny doesn't even want to imagine what Mrs. Gustafson will do to them if they get caught trying to steal her boxes. She'll probably make them take one thousand punishments from the black box each and every day for the rest of the school year. And even if they succeed, they'll have to run away from home and live on the streets. They would never feel safe again. The whole idea is so risky that Benny's beginning to think they might be making a terrible mistake.

But despite the hesitation, Benny finds himself saying, "Okay. Let's do it."

"Heck yeah!" Mika bounces up and down like a

beach ball. "Tomorrow night those boxes will be ours!"

Mika's enthusiasm is so infectious that Benny soon finds himself bouncing and cheering right alongside her.

As Benny and Mika celebrate their momentous decision, a small group of super kids come up behind them.

"What are you freaks up to now?" Amanda asks them.

The two outcasts turn around to see her approaching with Billy and Matty at her sides. The two boys cower behind Amanda, hoping she'll protect them from the scary blob girl. Because of her fire powers, she's the only one brave enough to stand up to Mika. All the other super kids stay back by at least thirty feet.

"None of your business, *Hag*oness," Mika says.

As Mika oozes toward her ex-best friend, Benny tries to hide the ten combination locks at his feet by burying them in the sand with the heel of his shoe.

"That's *Dragoness* to you, She Blob," Amanda says. "I'm the super squad's fire-breathing champion and I'm not afraid of you."

Mika leans her gelatin head toward Amanda, stretching her slime body out to twice that of a normal human's.

"You're *really* not afraid of me?" Mika asks, getting right in her ex-friend's face.

Amanda backs up a little, but doesn't stand down. "No. I can breathe fire. I'll burn you to ashes."

Mika laughs. "You do realize that slime is mostly

water, right? I'll extinguish any fire you spray at me."

"N-no…" Dragoness stutters. She breaks eye contact and looks back at the others, not sure if what Mika says is true or not. Who says that fire can't burn slime?

"No, you won't," she says. "I can burn anything."

Mika just shrugs. "Yeah? Well, go ahead and try it. See what happens."

Dragoness doesn't act on her threat. Instead, she turns her attention to Benny. "Or maybe I'll just burn your *boyfriend*."

Matty and Billy burst into laughter when she calls Benny Mika's boyfriend. They high five each other behind Amanda's back and point at the slug boy. They think there wasn't a better insult their champion could have given Mika.

But the both go quiet as Mika yells, "You better stay the fuck away from him, bitch! If I even see you looking at him weird I'll melt that stupid face of yours right off of your head!"

A smug little smirk appears on Amanda's face. She realizes she hit a nerve by threatening Mika's friend.

"Oh yeah?" says Dragoness.

She opens her mouth and takes a deep inhalation, aiming right in Benny's direction. It's obvious she plans to just spray a burst of flames over the slug boy's head, just to scare them a little, but Mika doesn't treat it as a mere warning. She reacts just as quickly as she would if Benny really was in immediate danger.

A blue slime hand darts out of Mika's chest and slams into her ex-friend's mouth before a single flame can be released. Amanda's eyes shoot wide open at the warm goo covering her lips and nose. She tries exhaling her flames, but they won't come out. The lack of oxygen extinguishes the flames in her throat and Amanda quickly realizes she can't breathe.

As Amanda struggles for oxygen, Mika draws her in closer and says, "I told you to stay the fuck away from him, you stupid ugly cheating loser."

The two super boys are no longer laughing. They back away from their ex-champion, praying that the blob girl doesn't do the same thing to them.

"You did this to me, Amanda," Mika says, inches away from the girl's face. "You lied to the teacher and turned me into this."

Amanda tries to free herself. She grabs at Mika's slime hand but there's nothing there to grip. Her fingers just fall through, sinking into the acidic ooze.

"I should just end you right here and now," Mika says.

Her blue goo slides farther up Amanda's face, up over her hair and down her neck until her entire head is smothered inside a bubble of ooze.

"It's not like you don't deserve it…"

Benny doesn't know what to do. Mika seems mad. Really mad. It doesn't seem like she's just threatening her ex-friend anymore. He wonders if she's really going to kill Amanda. She could if she wanted to and Mika definitely looks like she wants to. It doesn't appear as though anyone else, not the teachers or other students, are going to do a thing to stop her. The only person who has the power to save Amanda now is him.

"Mika…" Benny says.

But before Mika can melt the girl's face off, an angel swoops down from the sky to save the day once again. Using her telekinetic power, Tracy pushes Amanda out of the slime so hard that she summersaults backwards three times and lands on her butt. Then the angel glides down to the sand and places herself between the superheroes and super villains in order to break up the fight.

"Why the hell did you do that, bitch?" Mika yells, turning her anger toward the angel. "I was just teaching her a lesson."

Tracy lowers her angel wings and turns to Mika and Benny. She doesn't explain herself to the slime girl. She just stares at them.

"We need to talk," Tracy tells them.

Benny realizes there's something weird about the look in her eyes. She's concerned about something and it has nothing to do with the feud between Mika and Amanda.

"What do you mean by that?" Mika asks.

She holds out her slime arms as though ready to attack the angel if she says the wrong thing.

"Your plan." Tracy looks at Benny and then back at Mika. "It won't work."

"Our plan?" Benny asks.

Tracy points at her head. "I can read minds. I have super hearing. I know all about how you two are planning to steal the boxes."

Benny and Mika look at each other, completely shocked by her words. They feel like they've been found out. Their plan has been foiled.

Mika doesn't know what to do but go on the attack. "And you think you're going to stop us?"

Tracy shakes her head. "No, the opposite. I want in."

Benny and Mika nearly fall over when she says this. "What?" Mika cries.

"I'll meet you at Benny's house after school," Tracy says. "We'll talk there."

And before either of them can say anything else, Tracy leaps into the air and flies off. She goes up into the clouds and disappears from their sight.

Mika turns to Benny and says, "What the hell?"

Even she's perplexed by this turn of events.

Behind them, Amanda gets to her feet and wipes sand from her butt. She glares at them, giving them a dirty look. But she doesn't just seem pissed off at the two of them. She also seems pissed off at Tracy. The angel is supposed to be her friend, part of the same clique of popular super kids, but Tracy doesn't appear to be on her side. Not only did Tracy save her in such a violent fashion, but she didn't beat up Amanda's enemies for her afterward. She suspects something is terribly wrong with that prissy angel-winged kid.

Mika glares back at her ex-friend until she returns to the others. Amanda doesn't worry her in the slightest. Tracy, on the other hand, could prove to be a problem.

"We'll hear her out," Mika tells Benny. She leans down and sucks the combination locks out of the sand, hiding them inside of her body. "But there's no way we can trust her."

Benny shrugs. He kind of likes the idea of having

Tracy's help. She's the smartest, prettiest girl in school.

"She's one of *them*," Mika says, nodding toward the team of superhero kids. "Not a super villain, like us. We should only work with other super villains."

Benny nods his head at his teammate, but he doesn't think he agrees with her. He's willing to welcome any help they can get, even if it's from their mortal enemies.

After school, it dawns on Benny that the girl of his dreams is coming over to his house. She's actually going to be in his room, seeing his things, talking to him and hanging out with him. This is both the most exciting and terrifying thing that's ever happened to him before.

Right when he gets home, Benny starts cleaning his room in a panic. He tosses all his dirty socks and underwear in the closet. He picks up all the Hot Pockets folders and TV dinner trays and puts them in a big green garbage bag.

Mika oozes into his room behind him with a frown on her face. "What the heck are you doing? You never cleaned up like this for me when I come over."

Benny shakes his head. "You're different."

"How am I different?" Mika asks.

"You mess up the place even more than I do. There's no point cleaning up when you come over."

Mika plops down on his couch and sprays blue goo across his wall. Half of a Spiderman t-shirt melts beneath her butt. "I don't mess anything up."

When Tracy arrives, she doesn't go to his parents' front door. She goes straight into the backyard to Benny's pool house, already knowing exactly where they would be waiting for her.

"Your superhero girlfriend is here," Mika says when Tracy knocks on the door.

Benny tries to clear his mind. He doesn't want Tracy to read his thoughts. It's almost impossible for him not to think about her, but he knows that it will be beyond embarrassing if she catches him in the act. As he answers the door, he tries to clear his thoughts of everything but the color blue.

Just blue. Just blue. Everything is blue.

"What is blue?" Tracy asks, as Benny opens the door.

Benny freaks out. She's already reading his mind. He doesn't know what to do.

"Nothing!" Benny says, trying to block out his thoughts. "Nothing is blue!"

In a defensive tone, Mika says, "*I'm* blue." She spreads herself out on the couch, trying to act cool. "You got a problem with that?"

Tracy dismisses the topic. She steps inside, closes the door and locks it. There's no place for her to sit with Mika taking up the whole couch, so she remains standing.

"You two are making a mistake," she tells them.

Mika oozes to her feet. "What do you mean by that? Are you trying to talk us out of stealing the boxes?"

Tracy shakes her head. "Not at all. I want to help you."

Mika slides closer. "And what makes you think we

74

need your help?"

Tracy's feathers ruffle a little. She looks them in the eyes.

"Do you really want to face Mrs. Gustafson on your own?" Tracy asks.

Mika and Benny look at each other. They don't understand what she means.

Tracy explains. "That's the main flaw in your plan. You assume that Mrs. Gustafson is like a normal teacher. You assume that she won't be in class at night or on weekends. But she'll be there. She's always there. She never leaves."

Benny can't believe what she's saying. "She just sleeps in the class?"

Tracy shakes her head. "She doesn't sleep. She just stands at the front of the class and waits until the next day. She doesn't bathe or change her clothes. She doesn't eat or use the bathroom. I don't think she's even human."

"That's impossible," Mika says. "How do you even know that?"

Tracy points at her head. "I can read thoughts. I've seen it in the minds of several of the other teachers and custodians. They're all scared of her. The janitors come in at night and see her standing in her classroom with the lights off, staring forward at the empty seats, completely silent. One of them even entered her classroom and asked what she was doing in the dark, but she wouldn't respond. Like she was some kind of robotic machine with the power switch turned off."

"Are you serious?" Benny asks.

Tracy nods. "I've tried to read her mind before, to understand what she really is. But there's nothing there. I don't know if she's able to block my power or if she doesn't even have a mind at all. Either way, she's a terrifying woman and you two should not dare try to steal her boxes alone."

Benny agrees. After hearing Tracy's story, he's even more terrified of Mrs. Gustafson than ever. He doubts he'll ever be able to build up the courage to steal the boxes now.

Mika doesn't seem to completely buy Tracy's story. She looks the angel up and down, trying to decipher what she might be up to, wondering if there might be some kind of hidden agenda for telling such an incredible tale.

"And you really expect us to believe all that?" Mika asks.

"It's the truth," Tracy says.

"And you still want to help us steal the boxes from her?"

Tracy nods her snowy head.

Mika crosses her slime arms. She still doesn't understand.

"But why?" she asks. "Why would you want to help us?"

"I want the boxes destroyed," Tracy says.

"What?" Mika explodes blue jelly all over the room. "Why would you of all people want them destroyed? Look at all the powerful gifts you've been given."

Tracy shakes her head. "Gifts? I don't think I've been given any gifts at all."

She spreads her wings and looks back at them over

her shoulder. "I see these as curses. Same as yours."

"Curses?" Mika asks. "Look at me. I'm a blob. *That's* a curse. You've got the powers of a god."

"That's part of the problem," Tracy says. "Life loses all meaning when you have the powers of a god. Everything becomes too easy. Too boring. With my powers of memory, I don't even need to bother learning anything anymore. I've read so many books now that I feel like I know almost everything there is to know on any subject. My power to read minds has made it annoying and pointless to socialize with other people. With my super speed, no one is able to compete with me in any of my favorite sports. And, with my telekinesis, I don't even have to get off the couch when I want something done. Nothing is a challenge anymore."

"But you can fly," Benny says. "It must be so much fun to be able to fly."

Tracy nods her head. "Yeah, it was for a while, but it's gotten old. Even flying loses its appeal eventually. Once you get used to being able to fly, it ruins walking for you, it ruins riding in a car. Those methods of transportation just seem tedious once you can fly, so you don't bother walking through the park on the way home from school or riding in the bus with your friends. Maybe if other people were able to fly with me it would be great, but it's lonely being the only person up there. It makes the world feel empty and small."

Mika just grumbles at her. The angel sounds like a stuck-up rich bitch to her, complaining about how oh-so-hard it is to have too much money, more than she knows what to do with. Where's the challenge in life when you already own everything you could ever possibly want? It makes Mika sick.

"But that's not the only problem with the boxes," Tracy says. "There's a lot more to them than that." She turns to Benny. "Whenever you put your hand in the bad box, do you ever feel anything happen to you besides receiving a curse? Like something is being taken from you?"

Benny thinks about it for a minute and then shrugs. "I don't know."

Tracy explains herself. "Whenever I gain a new power from the good box, I feel like it is taking away a part of me. A part of my soul. I don't feel like the same person anymore. Even though I have a photographic memory now, I feel like many of my memories from the past are disappearing. All the happy memories. I also feel like my emotions are becoming weaker. Food doesn't taste the same as it used to. Music no longer brings me joy. Comedies are never funny. I even feel as though I'm losing bits and pieces of my personality. I feel like I'm becoming a lifeless machine. I feel like I'm being erased."

When Tracy isn't looking, Mika glances over at Benny and makes a face at him as if saying *This bitch is fucking crazy!*

"That's not happening to you as well?" Tracy asks Benny.

She steps close to him, so close that he can smell her strawberry perfume. He tries not to think about her. All he can think about is kissing her when she's this close, but it's the absolute last thing he wants to think about.

Benny just shakes his head. "Not really."

She sighs, but Benny isn't sure if it's because she's disappointed by his answer or because she doesn't like what he's thinking about.

"Perhaps it's just the good box that steals souls then," Tracy says. "Either way, they should both be destroyed. They are both mechanisms of evil. We have to steal them and make sure no one uses them ever again."

Mika has had enough of the angel girl's bullshit. She gets in her face and says, "You actually think *we're* going to help you destroy the boxes? Hell no. You can destroy the bad box if you want but we're taking the good box for ourselves."

"You're making a mistake," Tracy says. "But, if you insist, after we remove our curses I'll let you take as many powers from the good box as you want…as long as we destroy it after that."

Benny and Mika look at each other, wondering about what they should do. Benny thinks it's a fine compromise if that's what it will take to get Tracy on their side, but Mika's not convinced.

"So what do you think?" Tracy asks them. "Will you let me join your super villain team or do I have to do it all by myself?"

Benny nods in agreement. "I vote her in."

Mika's smooth ball-head twists at Benny, as though sneering at him. She doesn't like how easily her partner is willing to cave in to the leader of the superheroes.

"I still don't trust her…" Mika says.

She thinks about it for a moment, looking at the angel girl and back at the slug boy with the stupid smile on his face. It's obvious Mika wants to refuse but doesn't seem capable of finding a good excuse to refuse her.

After a few minutes of silence, Mika says, "Fine. We can work together."

Benny raises his eyebrows in excitement.

"But this doesn't mean that she's a member of the League of Super Villains," Mika says. "We'll just call this a *temporary* alliance."

Benny and Tracy both agree.

"That works for me," Tracy says, flapping her angel wings so hard that it blows several of Benny's comic books off the shelves. "As long as I'm the team leader."

Mika just groans at the angel, wondering if she just made a very huge mistake. Even though she doesn't want to work with Tracy, she feels like she doesn't have a choice. If Tracy plans to steal the boxes on her own, she might try to beat them to the punch. And if she destroys the boxes before their curses are lifted, Mika will be stuck a blob girl for the rest of her life. That's just not something she can allow to happen.

Now that they are all part of the same team, Mika, Benny, and Tracy begin to get serious about their plans. The three of them sit in a circle on Benny's floor, sitting on pillows and blankets and eating frozen egg rolls from a bowl. Tracy's wings are spread out like a long white cape across Benny's carpet. Mika's blue blob of a body leans back against the coffee table, jiggling like a Jell-O mold.

"So if Mrs. Gustafson never leaves the classroom, how are we going to get the boxes out?" Benny asks.

"Based on my research, there are only two occasions when Mrs. Gustafson leaves her classroom," Tracy says. "Staff meetings and special events."

"When are the staff meetings?" Mika asks.

"They happen on Mondays, during lunch. But I don't recommend trying to pull this off at that time." Tracy pops an egg roll in her mouth and wipes the grease on the feathers of one of her wings. "Besides it being difficult to break into the class during school hours, Mrs. Gustafson doesn't stay in the meetings for long. Ten minutes, tops. We'll have a much better chance if we wait for one of the special events."

"What events do you mean?" Benny asks.

"The only one I know about is the school dance next Friday," Tracy says. "Mrs. Gustafson volunteered to chaperone the event. It lasts for three hours, so we'll have plenty of time to get in and out before she knows what's happened."

Benny nods his head, but Mika seems confused by Tracy's words.

"Why would Mrs. Gustafson volunteer to chaperone a dance?" she asks. "If she never leaves the classroom, why wouldn't she just let another teacher do it?"

Tracy explains, "She seems to like to be with our class at any school function we might attend. You two weren't there, but she was at the school play two months ago. She went to my dance recital before that. I even heard that she ran a booth during the Halloween carnival. It's like she has no other reason to exist than being a teacher to us."

Benny shivers a little.

Mika stretches out her blob legs and says, "Then I guess the dance next Friday sounds like our best option."

Tracy nods her head. "It'll be a perfect opportunity. Because it's a school function, it won't raise any suspicions if we're caught on school grounds at night. We can attend the dance with the rest of the class and break away one at a time. Then regroup outside the fifth grade wing."

"Wait…" Benny says, suddenly getting nervous about the plan. "We're actually going to have to attend the dance?"

"That's right," Tracy says.

Benny trembles a little. "I've never been to a dance before. Aren't you only allowed to go if you bring a partner?"

Mika says, "Yeah, so what?"

Benny looks at the angel. He's always fantasized about going to a dance with her. Last year, when they used to sit next to each other and sometimes talked or joked around, Benny would have asked her to a dance for sure if fourth-graders were actually allowed to go to dances. And now that they do have dance events, he's become so out of Tracy's league that even the fantasy of going with her is beyond laughable. A smile creeps on his face when he thinks that maybe, just maybe, he'll be able to go with Tracy to the dance, even if it's just for pretend.

When he makes eye contact with her, Tracy seems to know exactly what he's thinking. She shuts him down immediately.

"The two of you will go as a couple," Tracy says.

"I'm going with Mika?" Benny asks.

His face droops down with disappointment. Of course it makes the most sense they would go together. Everyone knows they're the two outcasts in school. It would cause way too much of a commotion if the most popular kid in school showed up to the dance with Slug Boy.

"Yeah, you're going with me!" Mika says in an angry tone. "And you better wear your best suit. I'm not going to show up to a dance with no slob."

She seems almost annoyed when she notices Benny's dissatisfied expression about going to the dance with her. She might be a blob, but she still considers herself quite a catch.

"Who are you going to go with?" Benny asks Tracy.

Even if it won't be with him, he's still curious to know who.

The angel shrugs. "I don't know. I'll just ask whoever."

Mika bulges in excitement. "Oh! I know who you should go with!"

"Who?"

Mika bubbles and bounces. "Can you please ask Daniel from Class 5-B to the dance? Amanda would be so pissed! If you asked him, he'd ditch her for you in a second! It'll be so great!"

Tracy shrugs. "Yeah, sure. Whatever."

"Yes!" Mika hops up onto the coffee table and jiggles

in circles like it's some kind of victory dance. "Vengeance will be mine!"

Tracy sighs at the overexcited blob girl, wondering if it was the best idea for her to get involved in Mika's affairs.

"I might've been wrong about you, Cupid," Mika says. "Maybe there's a place in The League of Super Villains for you after all."

When Mika is finished with her little celebration, the three of them go back to business and continue planning the heist. They have exactly nine days to prepare. They might not have the most favorable conditions for achieving their goal, but it is essential that they succeed.

CHAPTER
SIX

As Benny shows up to the dance, all the other kids stare at him in disgust. None of them expected that he'd be there. Kids from the other fifth grade classes who rarely ever have to see or smell him are especially disturbed by his presence. They don't have to deal with any bad box kids in their classes.

Despite the looks of disgust on the other kids' faces, Benny actually thinks he looks rather handsome all things considered. He's wearing a black suit with a blue clip-on tie. His white button-up shirt is freshly ironed. His hair is combed neatly in a left part. His lizard tail and goat legs are hidden within a baggy pair of dress shorts and thigh-high black dress socks. He even has a pair of white gloves to cover up his slug fingers while dancing. And even though his date no longer possesses a sense of smell, he put on some fresh musky cologne strong enough to cover the eggy odors that permeate his body.

It doesn't matter what the other kids say, Benny thinks he looks rather dashing. This is his first dance, after all. Even though he's not seriously attending the event, he plans to make the most out of being there.

The dance is taking place in the gymnasium building, which is separated from the rest of the school by a large courtyard of multi-colored gravel and pavement walkways. Benny waits outside in his fancy attire, pacing up and down the courtyard near the front entrance. They won't let him in without a date. Middle-school couples pass him, walking hand-in-hand toward the entrance. He's beginning to feel awkward being out there all by himself.

When Mika finally arrives, she says, "Looking good, Slug Boy."

The sight of Mika is quite a shock. Benny barely even recognizes her. None of the students do. She's not in blob form anymore. She's not even a stick figure. Somehow Mika has been able to perfect the art of molding her blue gelatin body into that of a human. She has the exact proportions she did when she was a human girl. She has her old facial features. Her old short bob of hair. She has fingers and feet and eyes and nose and mouth, only it is all made of blue slime. Her eyes don't actually see. Her nose can't actually smell. But she's like an exact replica of old herself in Jell-O form.

She walks toward him on high-heeled shoes.

"Wow…" Benny says, practically speechless. "You look… beautiful."

Benny can't believe he actually said that about Mika, but he really means it. She's even wearing a dress—white with blue polka dots. It's made of some kind of indigestible material that dresses aren't normally made of, like plastic or rubber, but Benny thinks it looks really nice on her.

"Thanks." Mika smiles and steps closer to him. "I wanted it to be a surprise. I've been practicing my shape-molding skills all week."

"You've gotten great at it!" Benny says.

Mika blinks her slime eyes at him, trying to show off just how detailed she's been able to get with her shaping. She even has jelly eyelashes. Benny is beyond impressed.

"I wouldn't be able to dance if I came in my normal blob body," Mika says.

Benny nods his head.

All the other kids stop to stare at Mika. The kids from their class are confused about how she could take human shape when she used to be just a formless blob. The kids from other middle school classes who have never seen her before are astounded by the slime girl. To them, seeing her is like seeing a jellyfish in person for the very first time. They don't think she's pretty like Benny does, or even see her as human, but she's still a sight to behold.

Ignoring the kids that are beginning to crowd around them, Mika holds out her goopy hand and asks, "Shall we?"

Benny nods and takes her hand. He can feel her soft squishy flesh through his gloves. It reminds him a bit of a water balloon. As they walk toward the entrance, strolling hand-in-hand like the other couples, Benny realizes she's developed such control over her shaping ability that she no longer melts everything she touches by accident. It's like there's a thin outer layer of protective skin that holds all the acidic ooze inside. He's very proud of his blobby blue friend for pulling it off.

Once they enter the dancehall, they don't see Tracy anywhere in sight. Mika knows she'll be coming with Daniel. When the angel asked him to be her date to the dance, he agreed in an instant. It was priceless when Mika heard about how pissed it made Amanda. The Dragoness got so mad she breathed fire at his locker and turned all of his textbooks into ashes.

Mika sees Amanda is already there, sitting on a bench on the far side of the gym. The dragon girl had no choice but to come with Billy after Daniel dumped her. Although Billy is a popular kid and her superhero teammate, Amanda is obviously pissed to have him as her date to the dance. He's far from the most attractive boy in class.

"I guess we have some time to kill before the feathered princess arrives," Mika says. "We might as well get a few dances in before the real fun begins."

Benny gets a little bashful all of sudden and asks, "Are we really going to dance together?"

Mika doesn't bother giving a reply. She just says, "We have to put on a show, don't we?" And then pulls her freaky pretend-boyfriend onto the dance floor.

It's in the middle of a fast bopping pop song, so Benny doesn't have to deal with anything too intimate. Mika jiggles and bounces to the music, twisting her body in cartoonish postures that only a slime girl could achieve. She hops and spins as light as water, singing along to the lyrics. Dancing is the one thing Mika really enjoys since she was transformed into a blob. She was always into dancing, but in her new form she can move freely. It's limitless. She can do far more than the human body is normally capable of.

The infectious smile on Mika's face brings Benny into the spirit of things and he finds himself dancing fervently, enjoying it more than he ever has before. With his goat legs he's hardly able to keep up with his partner or even dance in beat with the music, but he finds himself having a good time.

All the kids watch them carefully, awestruck by the slime girl's moves. Some are amazed or impressed, while others are frightened or appalled. Either way, they are the stars of the dance at the moment and people can't stop talking about them. Benny has no idea how they are going to sneak out of there with so much attention on them.

As he dances, Benny makes eye contact with Mrs. Gustafson over Mika's shoulder. She is standing across the room, monitoring the event from the shadows. Her eyes tighten at him. Just like all the other kids around them, her attention is on the two freak kids in the center of the dance floor. Only she doesn't look at them with amazement or horror. She looks at them in disapproval, like she doesn't think the failing children should be allowed to attend the dance or have so much fun. Mika's blob form was meant to be a punishment, not a gift. She does not look in the least bit pleased that the girl is using her curse as a source of delight.

When the song is over, Benny and Mika laugh and hug, high on the endorphins caused by moving to such an upbeat song. Benny can't stop smiling. It was his first time dancing with a girl, even if it was only Mika. He feels good about himself, maybe a little confident for a change. But then the music changes tempo. The school DJ puts on a slow romantic ballad and all of the couples around them embrace each other.

Benny begins to leave the dance floor to head to a seat, thinking they are done and the dance is over. But Mika protests in annoyance.

"You're not *really* going to leave your date before a slow song are you?" Mika yells at him.

Benny turns around, a little confused. "You want to dance with me... *that* way?" He points at other couples.

"Of course," she says. "We *have* to. Slow songs are the whole point of taking a date to a school dance."

Not able to find a way out of it, Benny returns to his date. He hesitates once he reaches her, not really sure what to do or where to hold her. She has to take the clueless boy's hands and place them on her hips herself. Then she places her hands on his shoulders.

As they sway slowly to the music, turning in a slight circle, Benny feels beyond awkward. He stares into her translucent blue face, looking her right in the eyes even though they aren't really her eyes, trying not to step on her feet with his clonking goat hooves.

He's able to relax after a moment, taking deep breaths

to calm his anxiety. Once he's able to release his tension and focus on the dance, he notices how pleasant she feels against the palms of his hands. Even through his gloves, he can feel the warmth radiating from her body. Her hips are so soft and squishy against him. His slug fingers can sense the vibrations of her acidic fluids swishing and bubbling inside her as she moves. Dancing with Mika is not like anything Benny has ever experienced before.

The sensation is so relaxing that Benny finds his eyes drifting shut, his mind slipping into a wonderful dream. But when he realizes what he's doing he becomes nervous about crashing into the surrounding dancers, worried about stepping on Mika's feet. His eyes snap open and he looks around the room.

He finds himself saying, "Tracy still hasn't come yet. I wonder what's keeping her..."

"Shut up." Mika smacks him on the neck. "You're ruining the moment. I don't want to think about *her*."

"Sorry..." he says.

Mika sighs at him. The moment is already lost. She looks him in the eyes, wondering what he's thinking about.

"You really like her, don't you?" she asks.

Benny nods his head.

She smiles and says, "Who do you think is prettier, me or Tracy?"

"Ummm..." Benny hesitates for a second, but then decides to be honest with her. "Tracy."

She smacks him again, even harder this time. "You're supposed to lie, dumbass!"

"I'm sorry!" Benny cries. "I meant you!"

Mika shakes her head. "Too late. You already blew it."

Benny kicks himself for saying something so stupid to his date. Of course she wouldn't want him to be thinking of another girl while dancing with her. But even though Mika is upset with him, she doesn't break off the dance. She just squeezes him a little tighter around the neck.

As he looks at her, Benny thinks about whether he really does like Tracy better than Mika or not. He's been in love with Tracy for so long that he doesn't even think about other girls. He thinks of the angel as so perfect that he's blind to all of her flaws, which are likely numerous. Tracy might be the prettiest girl in school, but Mika is far more important to him. Even in her blob form, the sight of Mika puts a smile on his face the second he sees her every single day. She's his one and only friend and their friendship makes her the most beautiful girl in the world to him.

He decides to tell her, "I think you're really pretty, too. I used to think you were cute before you got punished by the bad box, but now I think you're even prettier."

Mika jiggles in offense. "You like me better as a blob! What the hell's wrong with you?"

"W-well…" Benny stutters. "I mean… You're blue. Blue is my favorite color. I think it's the *prettiest* color. And you're the bluest girl I've ever met."

Mika thinks about it and nods in approval. "That's right. Not even Tracy is bluer than me."

Benny hopes that was enough to save him from Mika's wrath.

Mika continues, "I also have smoother skin, better

fashion sense, more personality, a cuter voice, a prettier smile, shinier cheeks, longer eyelashes. I'm taller, lighter, more flexible and better at dancing, singing and oozing through cracks in doors."

Benny doesn't know how to respond to that but say, "Uh… Yeah, I totally agree."

She nods her head with contentment, glad her date has finally come to his senses and now understands exactly how lucky he is to be dancing with such an extraordinary catch.

Before Benny knows what is happening, Mika closes the embrace. She squishes her body against his, wrapping her arms around his neck, dancing with him in the way that real couples dance. Her cheek presses against his. Her chin on his shoulder. Benny puts his arms around her back and squeezes her tightly. It feels like he's hugging a giant water balloon. The areas of her flesh above and below his arms bulge out as he pulls her close. Her insides swish and sway, making a deep *gloop-gloop* noise with every step.

As they dance through the next slow song and the next, Benny wonders if getting cursed wasn't such a bad thing to happen to him after all. Without the bad box, he wouldn't have to deal with crickets under his skin or slugs ruining his handwriting, but he also would never have gotten to know Mika. He wonders if becoming her friend makes all of the painful, disgusting, horrible curses worthwhile.

Benny and Mika both forget why they're even at the dance until Tracy arrives with her date. A loud slapping sound echoes across the gymnasium, so loud it can be heard over the music. The commotion is what gets Benny and Mika's attention. They see Tracy and her date, Daniel, in a confrontation with a steaming mad Amanda who just clobbered her ex-boyfriend in front of everyone. Daniel rubs his bright-red cheek and tries to explain himself, but Amanda doesn't want to hear it. She wants it to be clear to everyone that she's the one breaking up with him and not the other way around.

Mika bursts into laughter and points a blue finger at Amanda, relishing in her ex-best friend's anguish. Billy joins in and pushes Daniel, standing up for his date even though she'd rather not have anything to do with him. The whole thing causes quite a scene and Mika is endlessly amused by it all.

Mrs. Gustafson is forced to step in. She cuts through the dance floor and approaches the angry children. When the teacher arrives to them, Tracy steps off to the side and looks across the room at Benny and Mika. She gives them a quick nod and then returns her attention back to her date.

"That's our cue," Mika says, pulling Benny off the dance floor.

With the teacher distracted, it's a perfect opportunity for the two of them to make their exit. Benny wonders if the angel knew something like this might happen.

Perhaps that's even why she agreed to go along with Mika's idea to ask Daniel to be her date. Everything is going even better than planned.

On the other side of the gym, Mika finds an exit removed from the sights of onlookers and pulls them through the door. Benny takes one look back before he leaves and sees Mrs. Gustafson dragging Billy and Amanda away from the rest of the students. She's still too busy to notice their escape.

Tracy and Daniel are not in trouble, however, and are now walking hand-in-hand onto the dance floor to have their first dance. Tracy wears an elegant white dress that shimmers like a rainbow in the multi-colored lights. Her angel wings stretch out so gloriously that it catches everyone's attention, making them forget all about what happened to the blob girl and her freaky date that previously captured their eyes.

When Mika notices Benny lingering in the doorway to catch a glimpse at the enchanting angel girl, she grabs him by the back of the collar and rips him outside. Then slams the door shut.

Mika leads him through the shadows of the courtyard toward the main building, moving quickly yet quietly, hoping they don't run into a janitor or security guard.

"Tracy will meet us over there," she says, pointing at the slides on the other side of the playground.

Benny follows her across the sand and under the slide closest to the fifth grade wing. It's dark and hidden. Even a security guard with a flashlight won't be able to spot them.

Once they are sitting down in the sand, Mika says, "Now we just have to wait for the angel to escape from the dance and we'll make our move."

Benny nods. His heart is racing. He can't believe they're actually going through with their plan. This is finally it. Succeed or fail, there's no turning back now.

As his eyes begin to adjust to the dark, Benny is able to relax a little. He takes a deep breath and imagines the color blue on the exhale. Just when he is starting to feel a little more composed, Mika drops a bomb on him.

She says, "By the way, we're totally stealing the good box from Tracy once we finish our mission. We're not going to let her destroy it."

"What?" Benny's heart goes back to racing. "But we promised we'd help her get rid of the boxes."

"Yeah, we're not doing that. The good box is way too valuable. We're going to get rich and powerful off of it." Mika snickers and folds her jiggly fingers together. "Besides, we're super villains. We totally have to betray the hero at the end."

Benny doesn't argue with the slime girl, but he really doesn't agree with her decision. He doesn't like the idea of turning on their teammate. Tracy's just trying to do good by destroying the boxes. She doesn't deserve their treachery. And if she puts up a fight against Mika, things could get incredibly ugly incredibly fast.

"You should sit closer to me," Mika says, tugging on Benny's shoulder. "We'll be harder to see that way."

He looks over at her. They're already pretty close. If he gets any closer he'll be sitting in her lap. But he squeezes all the way in until her gelatin body is squished against his left side.

After a moment of sitting in silence, their bodies pressed tightly together, Mika says, "I had a good time dancing with you."

Benny's pulse becomes rapid again. He can feel it jiggling Mika's flesh with each heartbeat.

"Me, too," Benny says.

She looks over at him, just inches from his cheek.

"You can kiss me if you want."

Benny is shocked to hear her say that. "What? You want me to kiss you?"

"I didn't say I *want* you to kiss me," she says, saving face in case he says no. She couldn't handle the blow to her ego if she was rejected by the slug boy. "I said that I'd *let* you kiss me if you want to."

His voice begins to tremble. "Really?"

"Well, we came to the dance together. That's what we're supposed to do."

Benny doesn't know how to respond. He thought the dance was all for show. He didn't know she was treating it as a real date.

"Besides," Mika continues, "if we get caught out here it will be a good excuse. They'll just think we sneaked away from the dance to make out with each other, not try to break into the school. It probably happens all the time."

Benny nods his head. Her reasoning sounds plausible.

"What if Tracy comes?" Benny asks. "She could be here any minute."

Mika huffs at him. "Just shut up and kiss me or forget about it."

Benny doesn't protest anymore. He leans in and presses his mouth awkwardly against hers. Her lips feel soft and squishy. Her cheeks and chin jiggle against his face. He doesn't know what it's supposed to feel like to kiss a girl, but he's pretty sure this isn't it. Normal girls don't have that human-shaped Jell-O mold texture that Mika has. His eyes are wide open. His lips are dry. He's not sure how long it's supposed to last. He assumes Mika is confused by his kissing technique by now and wonders what the hell he's even doing.

He counts to five and then releases her. But before he has a chance to pull back, Mika takes over. She grabs Benny by the back of his neck and practically swallows his face. It's a shock at first. Benny doesn't really know what's happening. She pushes open his lips and drives her long gelatin frog tongue practically down his throat. Her mouth doesn't have much of a taste to it. He imagines she would be the flavor of blue raspberry slushies, but the reality is closer to a mix between Vaseline and rubber surgical gloves.

Although it feels weird and wet and squishy and awkward, Benny decides to just go with it. He hugs her tightly to his body and allows her to suck on his tongue.

It's a lot messier than he thought it would be. Slime leaks down his cheeks and neck. The only real problem is that Mika's acidic saliva is beginning to melt off his taste buds and make his throat go numb.

When she finishes, Mika leans her head back and smiles at Benny. She wipes her blue slobber off of his neck and says, "Sorry. I forgot to tell you that I kiss with my mouth open."

Mika puts his hand in hers and looks out at the bright moonlit sky.

When he looks at her smiling gelatin expression, Benny wonders why she's so happy after kissing him. He thinks she just did it as a favor to be nice to him so that he wouldn't feel so bad about himself. But that doesn't explain why she would look so cheerful to be with him. Benny decides to confront her about it.

"Mika?" Benny asks. "Do you... like me?"

Mika rolls her jelly eyes, annoyed by the question.

"I don't know..." she says in a sarcastic tone. "I just danced with you and made out with you and later tonight I plan to leave my whole life and run away with you. What do you think?"

"So... you really do?" Benny asks.

She obviously doesn't want to spell it out, but he waits for an answer anyway. She has no choice but to say, "Yes, I admit it. I like you. Are you happy?"

Benny is excited to hear her say it, but also a little confused. He can't believe she's telling the truth. "But why would you like me? Everyone thinks I'm disgusting."

"Well, everyone thinks I'm a gross blob and you

still like me. Why don't you think I might feel the same way about you?"

"Because I have slug fingers." Benny raises his hands. "Because I have a lizard tail and goat legs and crickets crawling under my skin."

Mika shrugs. "Hey, nobody's perfect. The cricket thing I just try to forget about, but I think your fingers and tail and goat legs are kind of cool."

"You think my goat legs are cool?"

She pulls up his pant leg to show off his furry animal hoof. "Yeah. You're like a satyr from Greek mythology."

"Really?" Benny smiles.

"You also have a cute face and cute smile and cute eyes," she says. "The only thing I don't like is that you lack self-confidence and lack any kind of backbone. We're going to have to work on those things."

Benny nods. He understands the flaws in his character, but he never thought that his looks could be one of his strengths. He's beyond happy that she actually thinks he's cute.

But he worries about his lack of confidence. She might not like him anymore unless he tries to change that. He decides to start now by asking a question he never would have asked her before.

"Do you want me to be your boyfriend?"

She looks away from him for a moment, trying not to give in too easily.

"I'll tell you what…" she says. "If we succeed tonight and get the good box all to ourselves, then you can be my boyfriend forever."

"Really? Forever?"

"Yeah," she says. "But if you ever side with Tracy over me, or tell me you think any other girl is prettier even if it's a movie star or super model, then I'll annihilate you."

Benny nods his head, agreeing with the arrangement. He's not sure if she was literal or figurative when she said she'd annihilate him, but he's sure that it would be in his best interest if he never finds out.

CHAPTER
SEVEN

Tracy takes far more time getting out of the dance than expected. Mika and Benny wait for her for so long that they drift off to sleep together, holding each other, cuddling to keep warm.

Benny has the nicest dreams of being with Mika. She actually said that he could be her boyfriend forever. He really likes the sound of that. He dreams of being with her always. Dancing with her. Kissing her. Holding her hand. Talking about evil schemes. He just loves the idea of being wrapped up in her warmth, sleeping against her like a human-shaped water bed, feeling her fluids bubble and churn against him.

When he wakes up, Benny notices that Mika has lost her form a little. Her face is oozing down his cheek and neck. Her legs are widening out. Her feet leak out of her high-heeled shoes. It's kind of cute for him to see her this way. It's like she's a balloon that's deflating on top of him.

But then he notices one of his hands is deep inside of her thigh and has probably been in there for quite awhile. It's not just his hand, though. The entire left side of his body has been submerged into hers. When he looks closer, he notices something wrong with his arm. It's a lot thinner than it used to be. The slug fingers have disappeared. All he can see is bone.

When Benny pulls his hand out of Mika's thigh, all that's left is a skeleton arm. He looks at it for a second and then screams at the top of his lungs.

Mika shoots awake. Her face molds back together and then looks around, wondering what the heck is going on. When she sees Benny's skeletal arm she screams even louder than he is.

"You digested me!" Benny cries.

Mika screams in his face. "I totally didn't mean to!"

The two of them look down at the rest of Benny's body inside of her and keep screaming when they realize that all of his left side is in just as bad shape as his arm. Half his suit is gone and much of his flesh has been melted away. He can see rib bones sticking out of white meat.

"What do we do?" Benny cries.

"I don't know!"

Mika lifts herself off of Benny, revealing all the damage her body has done to him. He looks like regurgitated raw hamburger meat. He's missing so much tissue that Mika has no idea how he's still alive.

"I'm so sorry!" She tries excreting pieces of him out of her slime, not that it's possible to reattach any of it. "I didn't mean to fall asleep!"

"It burns so much! You're the worst girlfriend ever!"

"I'll fix this later, I promise!" Mika lifts him to his feet. "We have to go!"

"Go where?"

"To get the boxes, of course!"

Mika drags Benny across the playground toward the entrance to the fifth grade wing. Sand sticks to Benny's melted flesh as he's carried like a ragdoll.

"What about Tracy?" Benny asks between moans of agony. "We have to wait for Tracy."

"She never showed up," Mika says. "It's nine o'clock. The dance will be over soon. We have to do it on our own."

Benny's mind becomes fuzzy. "We should at least wait a little bit longer."

Mika shakes her head. "We need to finish our mission and get you to a hospital. Maybe the good box will even give me some kind of power that will let me save you."

Benny is beginning to become delirious from shock.

"I don't want to die…" he moans.

"You *won't* die!"

"Make sure to kiss me again before I die…"

"If we get through this I'll kiss you until your lips fall off."

"You're going to melt my lips off, too?"

"Just wait here while I open the door."

Mika leaves Benny on the sidewalk outside of the entrance. She removes her dress and shoes. Then she oozes through the cracks of the door and unlocks it from the other side. When Benny looks into the hallway, he realizes there are other people inside of there waiting for them. The slime girl doesn't notice them before he does.

He points at them to warn the slime girl but with all of his pain and lack of strength he doesn't alert her in time. They're able to ambush Mika before she knows what's hit her.

A cloud of flames envelops Mika from behind as Amanda and her super team step forward. The blob girl turns into a sizzling ball of fire and crumbles to the ground.

Dragoness snickers in triumph as she walks toward them. "I told you slime can burn, you blobby bitch."

Benny can't see Mika in the flames. She has been reduced to a formless globule, releasing a blanket of foul smoke that covers the room. It smells of burning rubber. He wonders if she's dead.

"What did you do?" Benny cries.

Amanda turns her attention to Slug Boy and laughs at the horrified look in his eyes. Billy and Matty high five each other behind her.

"Mrs. Gustafson said you two were planning to break in here tonight," she explains. "She said that she'd give each of us *two* free gifts from the good box if we stopped you."

"But you didn't have to kill her!" Benny says, staggering into the hallway toward Mika's scorching remains.

"Mrs. Gustafson said we can use lethal force if we

needed to. And I *needed* to. Mika deserves to burn for being such a bitch to me."

"And you're next, Cricket Boy!" Billy says, stepping toward him. "You don't have your slime girlfriend to protect you anymore."

Billy stretches out an arm as he approaches, turning it into a hangman's noose of human flesh. He twirls it around, teasing the slug boy with it, a sinister smile curling on his lips.

But as he passes the burning blob, Billy doesn't notice that it has started moving again. It bubbles and twists, oozing in his direction. He doesn't realize she's coming for him until it's too late.

The burning blob rolls into his legs, sticking to him like a giant wad of gum. The flames ignite his dance suit. Not sure what the hell is happening to him, Billy looks down and notices that he's buried up to his knees in a pulsing sphere of magma. He screams as the blob curls itself around him, spreading the fire to the rest of his body. His entire suit lights up. His skin crackles.

Amanda and Matty are frozen in place, unable to act. They can no longer tell the difference between what is Billy and what is blob. They have no idea how they can save him.

In a last ditch effort to escape, Billy uses the full force of his stretching power. His neck elongates, extending ten feet behind him in order to keep at least his face out of the fire. His screams become distorted and high-pitched as his vocal chords stretch and become thinner. His arms shoot out of his burning coat sleeves like rubber bands, wrapping around light fixtures and water pipes that run along the ceiling. He tries pulling himself out of the burning mess, but the magma continues climbing up his limbs, slithering up his neck.

By the time the fiery slime reaches his face, Billy goes limp. He drops to the ground like a burning pile of yarn. Amanda shrieks at the warped look on her date's face as he dies.

"Billy!" Amanda cries.

The fiery blob squeezes back together into a ball and then turns itself inside out, extinguishing the fire in one quick motion. It grows back into the form of a human girl, only now with an extremely pissed off look on her face.

"You really fucked up this time, Amanda," Mika says.

Amanda panics at the look in Mika's gooey eyes. She can tell her ex-friend isn't fucking around anymore. She opens her mouth and shoots another cloud of fire at her.

This time, Mika doesn't go down. The fire encases her body, but she just turns herself inside-out to smother it. She doesn't even need to lose her human shape in order to pull it off. Amanda tries again with the same result. And again.

"Why won't you die!" she cries.

A claw of slime burst's from Mika's chest and slaps Amanda across the face so hard that it rips off a section of her cheek.

"You should have just left us alone," Mika says.

Amanda looks back at her with tears pouring from her eyes. She clutches at the meat dangling from the side of her face.

Mika steps closer. "Now you're going to have to pay."

Another slime claw shoots out of Mika's body and cuts through her forehead, tearing her scalp back to reveal a section of her skull. Blood gushes from the girl's wound, dying her blonde hair red.

"But Mika…" Amanda sniffs and sobs at her. "You're my best friend…"

Before she can say anything else, a massive blue tentacle whips through the air and slices her in half. It moves with such lightning-fast speed, such brutal force, that it is able to cut even meat and bone.

Amanda doesn't scream. Her pieces drop to the floor with a wet plop. Mika just steps over her remains like it's nothing but loose garbage as she continues down the hallway.

When Matty sees the slime girl coming toward him, his eyes fill with dread. He goes into ghost mode just before Mika swings a tentacle at him. The limb of goo passes through him and splats against a row of lockers. Then he runs away. He phases straight through a wall and escapes.

Mika turns back to Benny. "We need to hurry. He's probably on his way to tell Mrs. Gustafson about this."

Benny gets to his feet and staggers after her. He shudders as he passes the dead bodies of his ex-classmates. Neither of them resembles their former selves in the slightest. They now seem more like props from a low-budget horror movie, crudely designed out of rubber and latex.

He's just now realizing what a terrifying force of death and destruction Mika can be when she's angry. He always thought that calling herself a super villain was just a fun game to her. But now he wonders if she's serious. He wonders if she really wants to become a force of evil in the world, a fiend who won't hesitate to murder anyone and everyone who gets in her way.

When they get to the door to their classroom, Mika turns to Benny and says, "Will you still be able to crack the safe in your condition?"

Benny looks down at his skeletal arm dangling at his side and cringes, but he tries to hold strong. "I think so. I still have one good hand."

Mika nods. "Move fast. Remember your breathing. We can still get in and out before Mrs. Gustafson leaves the dance."

Benny agrees. When they're ready, Mika loses her shape and falls to the ground. Then she oozes under the door.

A minute passes.

Benny waits for Mika to open the door for him, but there's no sign of her. The door remains locked. He knocks but no one answers. He has no idea what could have gone wrong. There's no sound coming from the other side. It's like she just vanished. He doesn't know what to do but stand there and wait and pray.

Every second that passes feels like an eternity.

Tracy flies into the hallway. She pushes through the doors to the fifth grade wing and lands in the center of the carnage that Mika left behind. There's not much emotion in her eyes when she sees the mutilated corpses of her dead classmates, as though she already knew about them before arriving. Perhaps she read Matty's mind as he ran back to the dance.

When the angel notices Benny, she goes toward him and asks, "What happened? Where's Mika?"

Benny points at the door. "She went in there but didn't come back out."

Tracy doesn't need to listen to his answer. She was able to pull all the information from his mind the second she asked the question. She doesn't even need an explanation for the condition of his body.

"I was worried about this," she says, stopping in front of the door.

"Where were you?" Benny's voice is in a panic, but he's also relieved that Tracy's there to help him.

"You two should have waited for me."

"But you took so long. We didn't know what else to do."

She nods. "I was busy dealing with Mrs. Gustafson."

"You stopped her? She's not coming?"

"She's dead," Tracy says.

Benny's eyes light up with excitement. He feels relieved at the news. He feels like they're finally safe. If the teacher is gone they don't have anything to worry about.

Tracy looks at him with a serious face. "The problem is she's not the only one."

Benny doesn't understand what she means by that. He waits for her to explain, but she doesn't respond.

She holds out her arm and pushes him away from the entrance. "Stand back."

With a burst of telekinetic power, the angel blows the door off the hinges. It flies across the classroom and crashes into a row of empty desks. There's no sign of Mika within. The room is pitch dark.

When Benny peeks his head inside the room, he sees a figure standing in front of the whiteboard. Completely quiet. Motionless. It just stands there in the shadows, waiting for a new class to begin.

Benny turns back to Tracy with a puzzled look in his eyes, wondering what the hell is going on. But she doesn't need to spell it out for him.

There are two Mrs. Gustafsons.

CHAPTER
EIGHT

When Benny flips the light switch, he finds Mika standing off to the side of the room. She is facing their teacher, but she isn't moving. Her flesh is no longer translucent—now cloudy and white. Benny goes to her and rubs a slug finger down her shoulder. She doesn't respond. The skin is cold. Rock hard. The slime girl has become frozen solid.

Tracy walks past him and faces the teacher. She spreads out her wings and crosses her arms. Light emanates off of her like an emissary of all that is holy and good. She has the presence of a true superhero, of an avenger of justice.

Life enters Mrs. Gustafson's eyes. She blinks twice, coming out of her *off* mode. She gives her students the look of an average fifth grade teacher, acting as if it's just another class in session.

"Take your seats, children," she says to them. "We have much to go over in this short amount of time."

Neither Tracy nor Benny take their seats. They just stare at her. Benny is incredibly confused by his teacher's casual tone. When she notices they have no interest in listening to her instructions, Mrs. Gustafson pushes her horn-rimmed glasses up her nose and looks Tracy directly in her eyes.

"So you've come for the boxes I see," she says. "Both the good and the bad."

"I've come to destroy them," Tracy says.

The teacher nods. "I see. Then you have come to me as a true agent of good, have you? Very remarkable. I would expect no less from my star pupil."

Both Benny and Tracy are confused by her words. They look at each other. Even though Tracy has the ability to read minds, she can't get a read on her teacher at all. Everything about her is a complete mystery.

Mrs. Gustafson continues. "You're absolutely correct in your assessment. The boxes do pose a threat to the harmony of this world. They do not belong here. Their existence will bring nothing but chaos."

Tracy is confused. She relaxes her wings. "Then why do you use them?"

"I want to speed up the division between good and evil. I want to make it clear which is which early in a child's development. I believe it will be much easier on society if those who are good and those who are evil recognize their place before adulthood. It would set those who are righteous on the correct path so they will know exactly how to handle those who have fallen astray."

Tracy looks back at Benny. "Those who have fallen astray?"

"The dregs of society," the teacher explains. "Those who seek to cheat and steal and murder for their own personal gain. These types of people deserve to be singled out and recognized so that they can be eradicated by the virtuous."

Benny interjects, "But the tests aren't based on who is good and who is evil. It is based on who is the best at taking tests. You make it impossible for those who have failed to ever succeed."

Mrs. Gustafson sneers at the slug boy. She doesn't appreciate him interrupting the lecture with her star pupil.

She responds with a shrug, "People who are stupid, who are unfortunate, who are insecure, who are evil… They all result in the same thing. They are all misfits who feel the need to *take* in order to thrive."

"But what about Amanda?" Tracy asks. "She cheated on your test. She lied about Mika's involvement with cheating. Yet you rewarded her."

Mrs. Gustafson looks at her with cold dead eyes. "Cheating and getting away with it is an important skill for the righteous. A good cheater can elevate a capitalist society in a way that benefits even the meekest of citizens. Cheating is not the same as villainy. Only those who fail at it turn out wrong."

She looks at Benny and he cowers behind the frozen statue of Mika. Even though the slime girl is now ice, he still goes to her for protection. He presses himself up against her, wrapping his arms around her waist.

"But what is it that makes Benny wrong?" Tracy asks. "I've looked into his mind and he is a good person. Far better than most in your class."

"He is a bad seed," says the teacher. "If he sat through my class and accepted all of his punishments I would have released him from his curses by the end of the school year. It would have proven that he is obedient and accepted his place in the world. But here he is, attempting to steal the good box for himself, trying to get ahead in the world by taking what isn't his. Perhaps it is because he was seduced by a classmate using him as a means to her own gains, but the result is all the same. He has embraced villainy and it will be his ruin."

When she glances at Benny, he does not release his embrace of Mika.

"I have copies of me all around the world," says Mrs. Gustafson. "In every fifth grade class this year, in every school in every district in every country, I am teaching my lesson. I want you all to know which of you are worth saving and which of you should be expelled. I want your world to blossom and reject that which is holding you back."

Benny realizes that his body warmth is melting the ice statue of Mika. Three tablespoons of blue slime roll down her back and poke him in the stomach, trying to get his attention. They want him to keep going. They want him to defrost the rest of her.

"It is people like you, Tracy, who I designed these tests for. It is you who will step up and save this world. You will usher in a new era of change and enlightenment. You are my Abraham Lincoln. My John F. Kennedy. You care so much for the unfortunate, the oppressed, the victims of unfair treatment that you will give up everything in order to help them. That is why you have passed my ultimate test. Because of this, I will allow you to keep all of the gifts that the good box has given you. With them, you will set this world straight. You will bring your people into a new era of prosperity."

Benny's warmth has opened up a cavity in Mika's back, releasing a gallon of blue goo that shifts and pulses against his belly. The ball of slime begins to rotate and spin, causing enough friction to melt more of her frozen insides.

"I do not want your gifts," Tracy says. "The good box has taken from me. I feel it killing my emotions and making me less of who I was."

"That is by design," the teacher says. "Emotions make you act irrationally, more prone to abuse your powers for selfish gain. Saviors such as yourself must be unbiased champions of what is right. If you must choose between what's best for the world and what's best for you or who you love, you must choose the world without hesitation."

The cavity in Mika's back expands down into her pelvis and up into her skull as the blue slime moves rapidly within. Because the front of Mika's body is still frozen, Mrs. Gustafson doesn't realize any of her has been defrosted at all. Tracy just has to keep the teacher talking.

"But what of Benny and Mika?" Tracy asks. "Do you plan to put them back to how they were before? Can you heal Benny's wounds and thaw Mika from her frozen state?"

The teacher lets out a mechanical sigh. "Unfortunately, no. As you have passed my ultimate test, they have failed. And the failures are beyond redemption. They must be eliminated, cut out like an infection before it festers and kills your world."

When there is a good amount of Mika defrosted, a thin rope of slime crawls down the back of her legs. It coils around the desks and moves stealthily toward the front of the class.

"You made them who they are. It is your fault. They don't deserve to die because of what you did to them."

The trail of slime collects into a ball behind the teacher's desk. It reforms into a miniature version of Mika and waves back at Benny.

"They are exactly what they always would have become. I only sped up their progress toward corruption. Now that we know their true disposition early in their lives we can eradicate them before they cause a negative impact on your world."

Tracy gets between Benny and the teacher. "I won't let you. I think you are the one who corrupted them. If you want to kill them then I think you are the evil force who must be eradicated."

The teacher sighs and shakes her head. "You're too young to understand, my star pupil. But this must be done. It is for the good of your world." Her eyes begin to grow red. "Now step aside."

Tracy doesn't move from her position as Mrs. Gustafson turns her attention to Benny. She holds her ground, ready to even give up her life in order to protect the innocent.

"Don't!" Tracy yells, raising her hands and stretching out her wings to block her misfit friends.

A tornado of black smoke coils around Mrs. Gustafson's arm as she points in Benny's direction. Benny hides behind Tracy, crouching down and covering his head. He cries out, begging for the angel's help.

Before Mrs. Gustafson can make her attack, a blue tentacle of slime shoots up at her from behind the teacher's desk. It moves so fast that not even Tracy sees it whipping through the air. It moves even faster than the one Mika used to cut Amanda in half.

But the teacher is not harmed. She catches the blue limb with her smoke-encased hand and squeezes it. Then proceeds with her own counterattack. The swirling sinister smoke moves up the teacher's arm and pierces into the slime. The brilliant cheerful blue color of the tentacle changes. It turns into a rotten, diseased green color. The slime hardens and crumbles. The disease creeps across the tentacle, spreading toward the miniature version of Mika hiding behind the desk.

"Let her go!" Tracy yells.

Mrs. Gustafson looks back at the angel just as Tracy releases a blast of her telekinetic power. The teacher flies back, releasing the slime girl's diseased arm. She is pushed with such force that her body is driven through the whiteboard and into the brick wall behind it.

Before the teacher can recover, Tracy releases a second attack. This time it crushes her body against the wall like bug beneath a flyswatter. Her bones are mashed inward. Her limbs flattened. Her glasses pushed all the way through her head. The only parts of her that still move are her fingers, twitching like the legs of a smashed cockroach.

Benny runs to Mika to make sure she's okay. She lost a bit of flesh in Mrs. Gustafson's attack, but it didn't harm the majority of her body. The rotten tentacle of slime has hardened into a black crust on the ground, unable to be reattached to the rest of her body.

"She doesn't bleed," Tracy says, stepping closer to examine their teacher's body.

The corpse of Mrs. Gustafson looks far from human. It leaks a white fluid from all the cracks in her crushed skull. She doesn't seem to have bones or organs inside of her. Her artificial flesh slides down a black exoskeleton. Her insides seem to consist exclusively of a creamy goo that emits a strong odor of banana and bacon grease.

Benny tries not to look at the teacher. She's always terrified him and always made him want to avoid eye contact. The fact that she's dead doesn't change anything. She still seems like a horrifying creature. She still seems dangerous. He keeps his distance from her smashed insect body, even though there's nothing else she can do to him ever again.

They all work together to melt Mika and bring her back to her original mass. The miniature version of Mika grows bigger with each ounce of slime that is reabsorbed into her. Once she is back to her old size, Benny gives her a hug, even with his skeletal arm.

"Fuck…" Mika says when she gets a good look at Benny's condition.

In the lighting of the classroom, she can now tell exactly

how much she damaged him on the playground. His flesh is still dripping off of his bones, melting apart like slow-roasted meat in a pressure cooker. Some of it continued to dissolve even after being separated from her slime, like the digestive acids had remained inside of his fibers and continued to liquefy him. He doesn't look like he could possibly pull through after all of this.

Mika feels terrible. She would never purposely hurt her one true friend in such a way. "We need to get you to a hospital. Fast."

But Tracy doesn't think it's very serious.

"He'll be fine," she says. "Forget about him."

"But he could die!" Mika says.

"If those wounds were to kill him he'd already be dead. But he's not as weak as a normal human anymore."

They look at her with confused expressions.

Tracy explains, "Because he's been cursed so much by the bad box, his body has become resilient to damage. He can survive injuries that would kill a normal human boy. He's become strong. Durable. Although he will be permanently scarred for life, he won't die. He doesn't even need to go to a hospital in order to pull through."

Mika looks at Benny, not able to believe or trust the angel's words. But Benny just nods back at her.

"The pain has mostly gone away," he says. "I think I'll be fine."

He lifts his skeletal arm and squeezes his fingers into a fist and then releases it. "I can even move it a little."

Mika frowns and hugs him. She feels terrible for what she did.

"We need to hurry," Tracy says. "The police will be here soon. We need to get the boxes and leave before they get here."

Mika looks at Benny, wondering if he's okay to crack the safe. He nods his head. It won't be a problem for him as long as he has friends who believe in him.

Benny bends down to the teacher's desk and cracks the combination lock in less than a minute. His remaining slug fingers know exactly what to do. When he opens the safe, the two boxes issue a loud humming noise that echoes through the classroom.

He pulls them out one at a time, first the bad box, then the good. He places them on top of the teacher's desk side-by-side and the room floods with a radiant glow—both malevolent and glorious.

The three children stare at the boxes for a moment, overwhelmed by their power. They feel the horrible evil of the bad box at the same time as the euphoric beauty of the good. It fills them with a combination of ecstasy and discomfort.

But before Mika can grab them, the boxes fly off of the table. They go to Tracy and hover by her side, held up by her telekinetic powers.

"I'm sorry, but I must take them both," the angel says. "I need to destroy them before they are ever used again."

Benny's jaw draws open with shock. "You said you would remove our curses once we got the boxes. You said we could have all the good box gifts that we wanted!"

Tracy shakes her head. "I'm sorry, but I can't let you use them. The good box will bring you nothing but misery."

Mika looks at Benny. "I told you we couldn't trust her."

Benny doesn't believe it. He begs the angel to reconsider. "But what about our curses? I don't want to be stuck this way for the rest of my life."

Tracy looks at him with pity but says, "You won't survive if I remove your curses now. They are the only thing that is keeping you alive. Both of you would die if you went back to how you were before."

"That's bullshit!" Mika cries.

Tracy frowns at her. "I'm sorry, but it's the truth. Get out of here before the police show up. I'll make sure they don't come after you."

But Mika isn't having any of it.

"You're just like the others." She steps toward her, anger swelling in her translucent eyes. "Give me those boxes or you won't live to regret it."

"It wouldn't be wise to fight me on this," Tracy tells her.

"Speak for yourself!"

Mika runs at the angel and swings a tentacle at her head. Even though it is as fast as the one that killed Amanda, Tracy is able to dodge it using her super speed.

"You don't want to do this," Tracy says.

Mika releases thirteen tentacles at her, one at a time, and Tracy dodges every one of them. The angel spins in a circle, ducks and jumps. Not a single one hits her. But the slime girl wasn't trying to hit the angel. She's just trying to distract her. Mika knows that Tracy can read minds, even the slime girl's brainless mind. In order to prevent her from using the mind-reading power, Mika is throwing everything at her at once. The angel must put all her efforts into her super speed if she doesn't want to be cut in half. The ability to read minds isn't enough to stop her.

Before Tracy knows what's happening, Mika opens her mouth and launches her frog tongue at her. The tongue seizes the glowing blue box hovering behind the angel's shoulder. Mika sucks it out of the air and swallows it, then oozes out of reach.

"Give it back," the angel says.

"It's mine now," Mika says, sliding toward the door. "Destroy the bad box if you want to, but we're keeping this." Mika looks at Benny and nods, trying to signal him that it's time they made their escape.

But the angel gets between them and the door in a snap of a finger, blocking their way out. They have to get through her if they want to leave.

She looks at Benny with her heavenly eyes and tries to plead with him. "Tell her to give it to me, Benny. There's no good that will come of resisting. Even if you get away with the box, it will only bring you to ruin."

Mika says, "Benny's on my side. You can't turn him against me."

Tracy shakes her head. "I see in his mind. He knows I'm right. Destroying the box is the wise thing to do."

"Bullshit!" Mika says. She looks at Benny. "Tell her you want the good box as much as I do."

Benny hesitates for a moment. He breaks eye contact. "Well, she might have a point..."

"Don't you dare tell me you agree with her," Mika says. "Whose side are you on, mine or hers?"

"Yours," he says.

"Then tell her to fuck off and get out of our way," Mika says.

Benny sighs. He doesn't like confrontation, especially not between two people he cares so much about.

He stands by Mika's side and tries to reason with the angel. "Tracy, please just let us through. This doesn't have to get ugly."

"It won't if you just hand over the box," Tracy says.

Benny says, "If you two fight seriously, one of you might die. I don't want either of you to die. The box doesn't matter as much as your lives do."

Tracy looks him up and down, wondering if she should give in.

"You're supposed to be a hero," Benny continues. "Wouldn't a hero rather prevent deaths than cause them? It's not a big deal if you let us take the box. It will still be gone. No one else in class will ever use it."

The angel looks over at the glowing box in Mika's body. She takes a moment to think, eying the box carefully. It's like she sees something inside of it that she never noticed before.

"I'll let you take it without a fight on one condition," Tracy says.

Benny is excited to hear this. He nods his head rapidly. "Yes, anything."

She points at the box inside of Mika. "You have to put your hand in the good box. One time each."

Benny and Mika look at each other. They don't understand why she would want them to do that. Stopping them from using it is exactly what she's been trying to prevent.

Mika shakes her head. "You just want to steal it from us once it's out in the open."

"That's not it," she says. "There's something I want to test." She points at the box. "I don't think it works anymore. I'm not sure if it ever worked at all."

The other two are confused. Of course the box works. Mika is sure she's pulling a trick.

Tracy continues, "Your slime has been inside of the box this whole time and you haven't gotten a single power. There's a chance that the box doesn't work without Mrs. Gustafson."

The angel is beginning to make sense to them. Mika wonders if she's right. She pulls out the box and puts her hand inside of it. Nothing happens. Benny tries and he doesn't get a power either. Just in case bad box kids aren't allowed to use the good box, Tracy puts her hand inside but it doesn't even work for her.

"What the hell!" Mika cries, throwing the box to the ground. "We did all of that for nothing!"

"At least you didn't kill each other over nothing..." Benny says.

Tracy lifts the box up off of the floor with her telekinetic power. "I still plan to destroy them. These things don't belong in our world."

"Let's just get the hell out of here before the cops show up," Mika says, pushing past Tracy and sliding into the hallway.

Benny and the angel follow after.

Outside the school, several police cars are parked out front. Their lights spinning, brightening the darkened school yard with red flashes. But there aren't any police officers to be seen. There also aren't any students on their way out of the dance. No parents waiting in their cars for their children to be finished.

The parking lot is dead empty. The place looks haunted. They have no idea where the cops could have gone, where the other kids went. Perhaps they were all inside the building or perhaps they all just ran away for some reason. It feels like time has stopped.

It begins to rain. Gently at first, and then harder.

"Something's here," Tracy says.

Benny and Mika look at each other.

"What is it?" Benny asks.

Tracy doesn't need to answer. They both see them standing on the far side of the parking lot. Hundreds of them. An army of Mrs. Gustafsons that just stare at them from behind the empty police cruisers.

"There's so many of them…" Benny says.

Mika oozes closer. "What do they want?"

"They want to kill the two of you and retrieve the

boxes," Tracy explains.

"So we have to fight them?" Mika asks. "*All* of them?"

Tracy shakes her head. "No, we run."

She steps forward and grows into a giantess, stretching a hundred feet off the ground. Mika and Benny stand behind her heels, sheltered from the rain by her massive canopy-like dress.

The angel stands over the army of teachers. With her enormous size and lightning speed, she could crush them all like cockroaches before they could do a thing to stop her. But Tracy is a hero. She doesn't kill needlessly.

She picks up Mika and Benny in each of her hands. Then she spreads her wings and flaps them with so much force they blow a hurricane across the school yard. The Mrs. Gustafsons just stare up at her in disappointment.

"You'll regret saving them," they all tell her.

Then the angel leaps off the ground and flies away.

More of the copies of Mrs. Gustafson surround Benny's house when they arrive. They surround Mika's and Tracy's houses as well. The three of them had packed bags just in case they needed to run away from home, but there's no way they can get them without a showdown with their teachers.

Tracy decides to leave all their belongings behind. She keeps flying. The Mrs. Gustafsons just stare at them as they pass by overhead, but they do nothing to stop them.

The three fly out of town. They cross the state border and then continue across the country. The angel has to take the two outcasts far away from danger, but has no idea where that would be.

After a few hours of travel, she drops them off at a farm house in the middle of nowhere, Wyoming. She lands quietly in a field of wheat and places her two classmates gently on the ground before shrinking back to her normal size.

The farmhouse is dimly lit. Whoever lives there is likely still awake.

"They're nice people," Tracy says, nodding toward the house. "They'll help you."

"How do you know?" Benny asks.

The mind-reader just taps her head in response. "You can either talk to them and ask for help or sleep in their barn and leave in the morning. You'll be fine either way."

Benny curls a slug through his bone arm.

"So you're just going to leave us here?" he asks.

"It's the only way to protect you."

"Where will you go?"

"I plan to find my own place somewhere in the countryside. Somewhere Mrs. Gustafson won't find me. Once I figure out a way to destroy the boxes, I'll track down all of Mrs. Gustafson's other classes and retrieve all the good boxes and bad boxes from every school in the country."

"Can't we help you?"

Tracy shakes her head. "You'd just get in the way. Besides, neither of you actually want to help me."

Benny looks back at Mika and she shrugs, not interested in aiding the angel's mission whatsoever. He lowers his head, ashamed that he too doesn't want to help. He's just too much of a coward to face Mrs. Gustafson ever again.

"I'm leaving now," says the angel, turning back and stepping through the field of wheat.

She doesn't even say goodbye. She just turns her back and steps away from them, her wings brushing against the wheat stalks.

"Good luck, Tracy!" Benny calls out to her.

"Call me Cupid. That's who I am now."

Then the angel leaps up into the air and flies away, gliding through the night sky like an owl on the hunt.

Left alone in the middle of nowhere, Mika and Benny look at each other, not sure what they should do. Benny asks the slime girl if they should knock on the door of the farmhouse and ask for help, but Mika doesn't like that idea. She doesn't trust strangers. They decide to stay in the barn for the night.

The barn is unlike what Benny imagined it would be. He expected a large open room full of piles of hay that he could use as a comfortable bed, but the barn is not very comfortable or welcoming at all. It is packed full of random machinery, tools, farm equipment, bags of fertilizer, pesticides, empty crates, rotten firewood and spider webs. Lots and lots of spider webs.

They climb through a broken window and huddle together in the only open section of the storage barn. The area is muddy and rocky and full of rusted screws and nails. The only blanket they find is an oil-caked tarp that doesn't do much to warm them from the drafty night air.

"This isn't very comfortable," Benny says.

Mika says, "It fucking sucks."

They just both stare forward, leaning back against a stack of crates, watching the rats crawl in and out of a metal bucket in the corner.

"Everything was for nothing." Mika spits a wad of slime at one of the rats. It pegs him right in the butt. "We didn't get the good box. We didn't get our curses removed. We don't have powers that will make us rich and successful. And yet we still had to run away from home. We still have to live in hiding even though we failed our mission."

The rat struggles and squeals as its hind quarters are dissolved by the slime girl's acidic spit. Mika just watches the rodent as it dies in agony, satisfied that she brought another creature such pain.

"What are we going to do?" Benny asks.

Mika shrugs. She seems defeated. It's not like her to just give up and resign to her fate.

Benny has to be the one to bring her spirits up for a change. "Cupid will come through for us. I think she'll defeat all the Mrs. Gustafsons in the world and destroy the boxes and make it so that we can go home again. We just have to wait until she succeeds."

"You're naive if you think she's going to make a

difference. We're not going home. We're never going to remove our curses and go back to the way we were. We have to accept this as our new reality and figure out where we are going to go from here."

They pause for a moment. Benny thinks about how they never should have tried to steal the boxes. Mrs. Gustafson said they would have gone back to normal at the end of the year if they just accepted their fate. All of this happened because they didn't want to play by the rules. Even if the rules were rigged against them, it still would have been better if they just continued as good obedient students.

"And where should we go?" Benny asks.

Mika thinks about it. Her face becomes serious. A dark look grows in her translucent gelatin eyes.

"I say we leave this barn and go into the farmhouse," she says. "I say we get rid of the people who live there and take all their money and sleep in their beds. If anyone comes to find them then we get rid of them, too."

Benny is shocked by her words. He doesn't believe she actually means it. She's a good person. The best person Benny has ever known. There's no way she really wants to go through with something so horrible.

"Tracy said the people who live here are good people. She said they'd help us if we just asked for it. We should just ask for money. We should just ask for a bed to sleep in."

"You actually think they would help?" Tracy asks. "Look at us. We're monsters. They'll call the police the second we knock on the door. They'll probably blow your head off with a shotgun."

Benny becomes frustrated with her. He doesn't know what she's becoming. A tear falls down his cheek. His voice becomes choked up. "I don't want to hurt anyone. That would be horrible. I don't want to do anything so horrible."

"But we're super villains. That's what we do."

"I don't want to be a super villain anymore. I want to be a hero. Like Tracy."

Mika bubbles with anger. "You promised you'd never take her side again. We're super villains. That's who we are now. We'll take whatever we want from whoever we want from here on out. We've got powers. No one can stop us."

Benny just pouts and sobs. He won't make eye contact with her.

"I won't do it," he says.

"You don't have to. I will."

He shakes his head. "I won't forgive you if you do."

Mika oozes in front of him, forcing him to look her in the eyes.

"Of course you'll forgive me. You're my boyfriend now, right? I'm going to be your girlfriend forever. We will always be by each other's side, no matter what."

Benny stares into her gelatinous eyes. The only good that has come out of all of this is Mika. He does want to be with her. He wants to be with her forever. If only he could convince her to be a better person.

"You have to love me no matter how ugly I become..." she says.

Then she kisses him. Her gooey, rubbery lips encase Benny's mouth. She puts her long frog tongue inside of him.

When she pulls back, he tells her, "I'll always love you."

Then they embrace. They forget all about their argument and just hold one another, feeling each other's warmth. Before they go to sleep, they wrap the tarp around Benny, keeping it between them so that Mika doesn't accidentally digest him again. They hold each other and let all their worries disappear. It is the best sensation Benny has felt all year. He's never felt more loved. Not by anyone. If he can just hold onto this feeling he can get through anything. He'll never have any regrets.

As Benny sleeps, Mika oozes out from beneath the tarp, careful not to wake her unconscious boyfriend. Benny wakes a little, but doesn't sit up. He keeps his eyes closed as he hears her slither across the barn and escape through the cracks in the wall.

He knows what she's doing. She is planning to go into the farmhouse and swallow all the people who live there one by one. She will digest them until there is nothing left, until all trace of them has vanished. There's no way anyone will know what has happened to them. No one but Benny and Tracy.

After that, there will be no going back for them.

They will be murderers. Criminals on the run. They will live a life of stealing and murdering people. With their skills, Mika and Benny can rob any jewelry store, any bank. No mere human, no police officer or security guard or soldier from the military will ever be able to do anything to stop them. They can defeat anyone who gets in their way.

Eventually the superheroes of the world will come after them. All the people like Tracy who have passed Mrs. Gustafson's ultimate test. They will be the only ones who are capable of standing up to the slug boy and the slime girl. But there will likely be other super villains by then. Others who escape and survive Mrs. Gustafson's punishment. Perhaps the villains will team up with Benny and Mika. Perhaps the heroes will team up with each other. Either way, there will be wars in this world unlike any wars that ever have been fought before.

Mrs. Gustafson was trying to eliminate evil from the world when she invented the good box and the bad box. But all she ended up doing was corrupting those who were already good.

At this very moment, Benny wants to get to his feet and race out of the barn and stop Mika from doing something so horrible that it will set her down a path of evil for the rest of her life. But after thinking of all the horrible things the bad box has done to him, after thinking about how unfair he was treated, how he was accused of cheating when he tried so hard, how his teacher never even wanted him to pass any of the tests in the first place, he thinks maybe his girlfriend has the right idea. Maybe this is the only course of action they have left to take. He starts to wonder if maybe he deserves to take what he wants from those more privileged than him. They have things so easy and he has things so hard. To hell with all of them.

As Benny lies there in the lowly mud, spiders building webs on the back of his neck, rusty nails stabbing him in the lower back, he decides that this really is the only option he has left. Like Mika, he has no choice but to accept the fact that he is nothing more than a product of the bad box.

BONUS SECTION

This is the part of the book where we would have published an afterword by the author but he insisted on drawing a comic strip instead for reasons we don't quite understand.

Thanks for reading my newest book, *The Bad Box*. It was a fun one to write.

It's me CM3!

So those of you who have met me in person might have realized that I don't actually look anything like I do in these comics.

I once resembled these drawings but that was a very long time ago. Not so much anymore.

For starters, I got Lasik eye surgery a while back and no longer need to wear glasses. So I look more like this:

I also think my sideburns look stupid without the glasses and often shave them off, to look like this:

And although I'm always smiling on the inside, you'll rarely ever see a smile on my face.

I also only wear an overcoat when it's cold out, which is pretty rare. I'm usually in a t-shirt.

My weight also changes drastically from time to time. I can gain or lose 50 pounds in a single month no problem, so it's normal for me to be fat one time you see me and skinny the next.

And sometimes I'm lazy and don't bother shaving my head and let my hair grow in crazy directions.

So yeah I just draw myself like this because it's more fun and I assume someday I'm going to look like this again.

I'm sure I'll need glasses again eventually and grow my sideburns out and look exactly like this.

Maybe by then I'll even be better at drawing cartoons and I'll be able to do a really accurate depiction of myself.

Like the version of me I created when I played the first Saints Row game.

Me in Saints Row:

3rd Street Saints *REPRESENT!*

THE
END

ABOUT THE AUTHOR

Carlton Mellick III is one of the leading authors of the bizarro fiction subgenre. Since 2001, his books have drawn an international cult following, despite the fact that they have been shunned by most libraries and chain bookstores.

He won the Wonderland Book Award for his novel, *Warrior Wolf Women of the Wasteland*, in 2009. His short fiction has appeared in *Vice Magazine, The Year's Best Fantasy and Horror #16, The Magazine of Bizarro Fiction,* and *Zombies: Encounters with the Hungry Dead*, among others. He is also a graduate of Clarion West, where he studied under the likes of Chuck Palahniuk, Connie Willis, and Cory Doctorow.

He lives in Portland, OR, the bizarro fiction mecca.

Visit him online at **www.carltonmellick.com**

STACKING DOLL

Benjamin never thought he'd ever fall in love with anyone, let alone a Matryoshkan, but from the moment he met Ynaria he knew she was the only one for him. Although relationships between humans and Matryoshkans are practically unheard of, the two are determined to get married despite objections from their friends and family. After meeting Ynaria's strict conservative parents, it becomes clear to Benjamin that the only way they will approve of their union is if they undergo The Trial—a matryoshkan wedding tradition where couples lock themselves in a house for several days in order to introduce each other to all of the people living inside of them.

SNUGGLE CLUB

After the death of his wife, Ray Parker decides to get involved with the local "cuddle party" community in order to once again feel the closeness of another human being. Although he's sure it will be a strange and awkward experience, he's determined to give anything a try if it will help him overcome his crippling loneliness. But he has no idea just how unsettling of an experience it will be until it's far too late to escape.

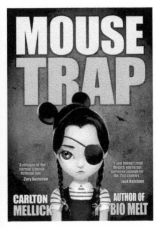

MOUSE TRAP

It's the last school trip young Emily will ever get to go on. Not because it's the end of the school year, but because the world is coming to an end. Teachers, parents, and other students have been slowly dying off over the past several months, killed in mysterious traps that have been appearing across the countryside. Nobody knows where the traps come from or who put them there, but they seem to be designed to exterminate the entirety of the human race.

Emily thought it was going to be an ordinary trip to the local amusement park, but what was supposed to be a normal afternoon of bumper cars and roller coasters has turned into a fight for survival after their teacher is horrifically killed in front of them, leaving the small children to fend for themselves in a life or death game of mouse and mouse trap.

NEVERDAY

Karl Lybeck has been repeating the same day over and over again, in a constant loop, for what feels like a thousand years. He thought he was the only person trapped in this eternal hell until he meets a young woman named January who is trapped in the same loop that Karl's been stuck within for so many centuries. But it turns out that Karl and January aren't alone. In fact, the majority of the population has been repeating the same day just as they have been. And society has mutated into something completely different from the world they once knew.

THE BOY WITH THE CHAINSAW HEART

Mark Knight awakens in the afterlife and discovers that he's been drafted into Hell's army, forced to fight against the hordes of murderous angels attacking from the North. He finds himself to be both the pilot and the fuel of a demonic war machine known as Lynx, a living demon woman with the ability to mutate into a weaponized battle suit that reflects the unique destructive force of a man's soul.

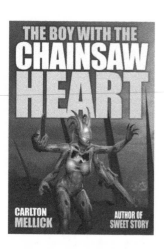

PARASITE MILK

Irving Rice has just arrived on the planet Kynaria to film an episode of the popular Travel Channel television series *Bizarre Foods with Andrew Zimmern: Intergalactic Edition*. Having never left his home state, let alone his home planet, Irving is hit with a severe case of culture shock. He's not prepared for Kynaria's mushroom cities, fungus-like citizens, or the giant insect wildlife. He's also not prepared for the consequences after he spends the night with a beautiful nymph-like alien woman who infects Irving with dangerous sexually-transmitted parasites that turn his otherworldly business trip into an agonizing fight for survival.

THE BIG MEAT

In the center of the city once known as Portland, Oregon, there lies a mountain of flesh. Hundreds of thousands of tons of rotting flesh. It has filled the city with disease and dead-lizard stench, contaminated the water supply with its greasy putrid fluids, clogged the air with toxic gasses so thick that you can't leave your house without the aid of a gas mask. And no one really knows quite what to do about it. A thousand-man demolition crew has been trying to clear it out one piece at a time, but after three months of work they've barely made a dent. And then there's the junkies who have started burrowing into the monster's guts, searching for a drug produced by its fire glands, setting back the excavation even longer.

It seems like the corpse will never go away. And with the quarantine still in place, we're not even allowed to leave. We're stuck in this disgusting rotten hell forever.

THE TERRIBLE THING THAT HAPPENS

There is a grocery store. The last grocery store in the world. It stands alone in the middle of a vast wasteland that was once our world. The open sign is still illuminated, brightening the black landscape. It can be seen from miles away, even through the poisonous red ash. Every night at the exact same time, the store comes alive. It becomes exactly as it was before the world ended. Its shelves are replenished with fresh food and water. Ghostly shoppers walk the aisles. The scent of freshly baked breads can be smelled from the rust-caked parking lot. For generations, a small community of survivors, hideously mutated from the toxic atmosphere, have survived by collecting goods from the store. But it is not an easy task. Decades ago, before the world was destroyed, there was a terrible thing that happened in this place. A group of armed men in brown paper masks descended on the shopping center, massacring everyone in sight. This horrible event reoccurs every night, in the exact same manner. And the only way the wastelanders can gather enough food for their survival is to traverse the killing spree, memorize the patterns, and pray they can escape the bloodbath in tact.

BIO MELT

Nobody goes into the Wire District anymore. The place is an industrial wasteland of poisonous gas clouds and lakes of toxic sludge. The machines are still running, the drone-operated factories are still spewing biochemical fumes over the city, but the place has lain abandoned for decades.

When the area becomes flooded by a mysterious black ooze, six strangers find themselves trapped in the Wire District with no chance of escape or rescue.

EVER TIME WE MEET AT THE DAIRY QUEEN, YOUR WHOLE FUCKING FACE EXPLODES

Ethan is in love with the weird girl in school. The one with the twitchy eyes and spiders in her hair. The one who can't sit still for even a minute and speaks in an odd squeaky voice. The one they call Spiderweb.

Although she scares all the other kids in school, Ethan thinks Spiderweb is the cutest, sweetest, most perfect girl in the world. But there's a problem. Whenever they go on a date at the Dairy Queen, her whole fucking face explodes.

EXERCISE BIKE

There is something wrong with Tori Manetti's new exercise bike. It is made from flesh and bone. It eats and breathes and poops. It was once a billionaire named Darren Oscarson who underwent years of cosmetic surgery to be transformed into a human exercise bike so that he could live out his deepest sexual fantasy. Now Tori is forced to ride him, use him as a normal piece of exercise equipment, no matter how grotesque his appearance.

SPIDER BUNNY

Only Petey remembers the Fruit Fun cereal commercials of the 1980s. He remembers how warped and disturbing they were. He remembers the lumpy-shaped cartoon children sitting around a breakfast table, eating puffy pink cereal brought to them by the distortedly animated mascot, Berry Bunny. The characters were creepier than the Sesame Street Humpty Dumpty, freakier than Mr. Noseybonk from the old BBC show Jigsaw. They used to give him nightmares as a child. Nightmares where Berry Bunny would reach out of the television and grab him, pulling him into her cereal bowl to be eaten by the demented cartoon children.

When Petey brings up Fruit Fun to his friends, none of them have any idea what he's talking about. They've never heard of the cereal or seen the commercials before. And they're not the only ones. Nobody has ever heard of it. There's not even any information about Fruit Fun on google or wikipedia. At first, Petey thinks he's going crazy. He wonders if all of those commercials were real or just false memories. But then he starts seeing them again. Berry Bunny appears on his television, promoting Fruit Fun cereal in her squeaky unsettling voice. And the next thing Petey knows, he and his friends are sucked into the cereal commercial and forced to survive in a surreal world populated by cartoon characters made flesh.

SWEET STORY

Sally is an odd little girl. It's not because she dresses as if she's from the Edwardian era or spends most of her time playing with creepy talking dolls. It's because she chases rainbows as if they were butterflies. She believes that if she finds the end of the rainbow then magical things will happen to her--leprechauns will shower her with gold and fairies will grant her every wish. But when she actually does find the end of a rainbow one day, and is given the opportunity to wish for whatever she wants, Sally asks for something that she believes will bring joy to children all over the world. She wishes that it would rain candy forever. She had no idea that her innocent wish would lead to the extinction of all life on earth.

TUMOR FRUIT

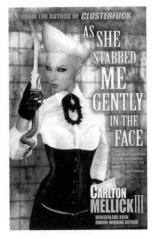

Eight desperate castaways find themselves stranded on a mysterious deserted island. They are surrounded by poisonous blue plants and an ocean made of acid. Ravenous creatures lurk in the toxic jungle. The ghostly sound of crying babies can be heard on the wind.

Once they realize the rescue ships aren't coming, the eight castaways must band together in order to survive in this inhospitable environment. But survival might not be possible. The air they breathe is lethal, there is no shelter from the elements, and the only food they have to consume is the colorful squid-shaped tumors that grow from a mentally disturbed woman's body.

AS SHE STABBED ME GENTLY IN THE FACE

Oksana Maslovskiy is an award-winning artist, an internationally adored fashion model, and one of the most infamous serial killers this country has ever known. She enjoys murdering pretty young men with a nine-inch blade, cutting them open and admiring their delicate insides. It's the only way she knows how to be intimate with another human being. But one day she meets a victim who cannot be killed. His name is Gabriel—a mysterious immortal being with a deep desire to save Oksana's soul. He makes her a deal: if she promises to never kill another person again, he'll become her eternal murder victim.

What at first seems like the perfect relationship for Oksana quickly devolves into a living nightmare when she discovers that Gabriel enjoys being killed by her just a little too much. He turns out to be obsessive, possessive, and paranoid that she might be murdering other men behind his back. And because he is unkillable, it's not going to be easy for Oksana to get rid of him.

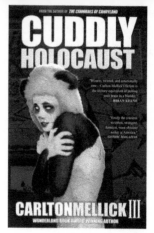

CUDDLY HOLOCAUST

Teddy bears, dollies, and little green soldiers—they've all had enough of you. They're sick of being treated like playthings for spoiled little brats. They have no rights, no property, no hope for a future of any kind. You've left them with no other option—in order to be free, they must exterminate the human race.

Julie is a human girl undergoing reconstructive surgery in order to become a stuffed animal. Her plan: to infiltrate enemy lines in order to save her family from the toy death camps. But when an army of plushy soldiers invade the underground bunker where she has taken refuge, Julie will be forced to move forward with her plan despite her transformation being not entirely complete.

ARMADILLO FISTS

A weird-as-hell gangster story set in a world where people drive giant mechanical dinosaurs instead of cars.

Her name is Psycho June Howard, aka Armadillo Fists, a woman who replaced both of her hands with living armadillos. She was once the most bloodthirsty fighter in the world of illegal underground boxing. But now she is on the run from a group of psychotic gangsters who believe she's responsible for the death of their boss. With the help of a stegosaurus driver named Mr. Fast Awesome—who thinks he is God's gift to women even though he doesn't have any arms or legs--June must do whatever it takes to escape her pursuers, even if she has to kill each and every one of them in the process.

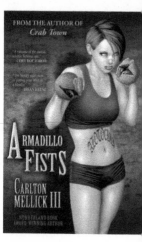

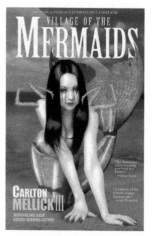

VILLAGE OF THE MERMAIDS

Mermaids are protected by the government under the Endangered Species Act, which means you aren't able to kill them even in self-defense. This is especially problematic if you happen to live in the isolated fishing village of Siren Cove, where there exists a healthy population of mermaids in the surrounding waters that view you as the main source of protein in their diet.

The only thing keeping these ravenous sea women at bay is the equally-dangerous supply of human livestock known as Food People. Normally, these "feeder humans" are enough to keep the mermaid population happy and well-fed. But in Siren Cove, the mermaids are avoiding the human livestock and have returned to hunting the frightened local fishermen. It is up to Doctor Black, an eccentric representative of the Food People Corporation, to investigate the matter and hopefully find a way to correct the mermaids' new eating patterns before the remaining villagers end up as fish food. But the more he digs, the more he discovers there are far stranger and more dangerous things than mermaids hidden in this ancient village by the sea.

I KNOCKED UP SATAN'S DAUGHTER

Jonathan Vandervoo lives a carefree life in a house made of legos, spending his days building lego sculptures and his nights getting drunk with his only friend—an alcoholic sumo wrestler named Shoji. It's a pleasant life with no responsibility, until the day he meets Lici. She's a soul-sucking demon from hell with red skin, glowing eyes, a forked tongue, and pointy red devil horns... and she claims to be nine months pregnant with Jonathan's baby.

Now Jonathan must do the right thing and marry the succubus or else her demonic family is going to rip his heart out through his ribcage and force him to endure the worst torture hell has to offer for the rest of eternity. But can Jonathan really love a fire-breathing, frog-eating, cold-blooded demoness? Or would eternal damnation be preferable? Either way, the big day is approaching. And once Jonathan's conservative Christian family learns their son is about to marry a spawn of Satan, it's going to be all-out war between demons and humans, with Jonathan and his hell-born bride caught in the middle.

KILL BALL

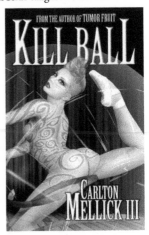

In a city where everyone lives inside of plastic bubbles, there is no such thing as intimacy. A husband can no longer kiss his wife. A mother can no longer hug her children. To do this would mean instant death. Ever since the disease swept across the globe, we have become isolated within our own personal plastic prison cells, rolling aimlessly through rubber streets in what are essentially man-sized hamster balls.

Colin Hinchcliff longs for the touch of another human being. He can't handle the loneliness, the confinement, and he's horribly claustrophobic. The only thing keeping him going is his unrequited love for an exotic dancer named Siren, a woman who has never seen his face, doesn't even know his name. But when The Kill Ball, a serial slasher in a black leather sphere, begins targeting women at Siren's club, Colin decides he has to do whatever it takes in order to protect her... even if he has to break out of his bubble and risk everything to do it.

THE TICK PEOPLE

They call it Gloom Town, but that isn't its real name. It is a sad city, the saddest of cities, a place so utterly depressing that even their ales are brewed with the most sorrow-filled tears. They built it on the back of a colossal mountain-sized animal, where its woeful citizens live like human fleas within the hairy, pulsing landscape. And those tasked with keeping the city in a state of constant melancholy are the Stressmen-a team of professional sadness-makers who are perpetually striving to invent new ways of causing absolute misery.

But for the Stressman known as Fernando Mendez, creating grief hasn't been so easy as of late. His ideas aren't effective anymore. His treatments are more likely to induce happiness than sadness. And if he wants to get back in the game, he's going to have to relearn the true meaning of despair.

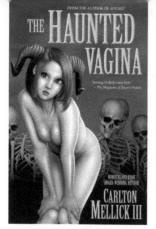

THE HAUNTED VAGINA

It's difficult to love a woman whose vagina is a gateway to the world of the dead...

Steve is madly in love with his eccentric girlfriend, Stacy. Unfortunately, their sex life has been suffering as of late, because Steve is worried about the odd noises that have been coming from Stacy's pubic region. She says that her vagina is haunted. She doesn't think it's that big of a deal. Steve, on the other hand, completely disagrees.

When a living corpse climbs out of her during an awkward night of sex, Stacy learns that her vagina is actually a doorway to another world. She persuades Steve to climb inside of her to explore this strange new place. But once inside, Steve finds it difficult to return... especially once he meets an oddly attractive woman named Fig, who lives within the lonely haunted world between Stacy's legs.

THE CANNIBALS OF CANDYLAND

There exists a race of cannibals who are made out of candy. They live in an underground world filled with lollipop forests and gumdrop goblins. During the day, while you are away at work, they come above ground and prowl our streets for food. Their prey: your children. They lure young boys and girls to them with their sweet scent and bright colorful candy coating, then rip them apart with razor sharp teeth and claws.

When he was a child, Franklin Pierce witnessed the death of his siblings at the hands of a candy woman with pink cotton candy hair. Since that day, the candy people have become his obsession. He has spent his entire life trying to prove that they exist. And after discovering the entrance to the underground world of the candy people, Franklin finds himself venturing into their sugary domain. His mission: capture one of them and bring it back, dead or alive.

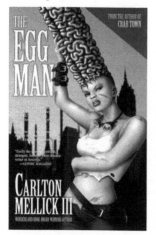

THE EGG MAN

It is a survival of the fittest world where humans reproduce like insects, children are the property of corporations, and having a ten-foot tall brain is a grotesque sexual fetish.

Lincoln has just been released into the world by the Georges Organization, a corporation that raises creative types. A Smell, he has little prospect of succeeding as a visual artist. But after he moves into the Henry Building, he meets Luci, the weird and grimy girl who lives across the hall. She is a Sight. She is also the most disgusting woman Lincoln has ever met. Little does he know, she will soon become his muse.

Now Luci's boyfriend is threatening to kill Lincoln, two rival corporations are preparing for war, and Luci is dragging him along to discover the truth about the mysterious egg man who lives next door. Only the strongest will survive in this tale of individuality, love, and mutilation.

APESHIT

Apeshit is Mellick's love letter to the great and terrible B-horror movie genre. Six trendy teenagers (three cheerleaders and three football players) go to an isolated cabin in the mountains for a weekend of drinking, partying, and crazy sex, only to find themselves in the middle of a life and death struggle against a horribly mutated psychotic freak that just won't stay dead. Mellick parodies this horror cliché and twists it into something deeper and stranger. It is the literary equivalent of a grindhouse film. It is a splatter punk's wet dream. It is perhaps one of the most fucked up books ever written.

If you are a fan of Takashi Miike, Evil Dead, early Peter Jackson, or Eurotrash horror, then you must read this book.

CLUSTERFUCK

A bunch of douchebag frat boys get trapped in a cave with subterranean cannibal mutants and try to survive not by using their wits but by following the bro code...

From master of bizarro fiction Carlton Mellick III, author of the international cult hits Satan Burger and Adolf in Wonderland, comes a violent and hilarious B movie in book form. Set in the same woods as Mellick's splatterpunk satire Apeshit, Clusterfuck follows Trent Chesterton, alpha bro, who has come up with what he thinks is a flawless plan to get laid. He invites three hot chicks and his three best bros on a weekend of extreme cave diving in a remote area known as Turtle Mountain, hoping to impress the ladies with his expert caving skills.

But things don't quite go as Trent planned. For starters, only one of the three chicks turns out to be remotely hot and she has no interest in him for some inexplicable reason. Then he ends up looking like a total dumbass when everyone learns he's never actually gone caving in his entire life. And to top it all off, he's the one to get blamed once they find themselves lost and trapped deep underground with no way to turn back and no possible chance of rescue. What's a bro to do? Sure he could win some points if he actually tried to save the ladies from the family of unkillable subterranean cannibal mutants hunting them for their flesh, but fuck that. No slam piece is worth that amount of effort. He'd much rather just use them as bait so that he can save himself.

THE BABY JESUS BUTT PLUG

Step into a dark and absurd world where human beings are slaves to corporations, people are photocopied instead of born, and the baby jesus is a very popular anal probe.

.